Girl with Flying Weapons

AYA LING

ISBN: 1494721961

ISBN-13: 978-1494721961

ACKNOWLEDGMENTS

A big thanks to my beta readers—Libertad, Victoria, Heather, and Kerrie for reading through the book in a very limited time! Also thanks to Clarissa, for listening patiently to my fussy demands on the cover. Finally, my heartfelt thanks to my friends and family for hearing me rant and complain throughout the tough writer's journey.

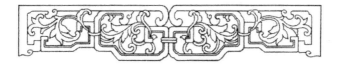

1

On a clear moonlit night, the Yang-tse River was aglow with several golden boats bedecked with flowing silk curtains and exquisitely painted windows. Laughter and cheers rang out as goblets were passed around and filled to the brim. For many of the rich and wealthy, nighttime offered a better excuse to be decadent, indolent, and free of social regulations. Although the Tang dynasty was now less prosperous than it used to be, the southern area, which was not wrecked by war, still retained some of its former splendour.

On one of the biggest boats, melodious music was dripping through the air, as intoxicating and sweet as the ruby red wine poured into semi-transparent goblets. A courtesan, around the age of eighteen, sat on the rear of the boat, her head modestly bowed, her long slender fingers moving on the lute. Her makeup was done in the latest fashion—cheeks powdered with ceruse, eyebrows painted in indigo blue, a beauty mark in the shape of a crescent moon drawn on her forehead. Her midnight-black hair was pinned up like a small mountain, and adorned with several golden hairpins. Large, luminous pearls glowed on her earlobes.

She was beautiful, though by no means outstanding. Her lute music, however, was extraordinary.

When she finished the song and bowed, the applause was tumultuous.

"Another song! Another one!"

A man who looked about fifty waddled through the audience. A few had to stand aside for him to pass; the man was clearly drunk. Drops of wine splashed down his front and dripped on the floor. Yet no one dared to tell him off.

It was Chu, the richest businessman in Yangzhou city. He made a fortune producing and selling salt. As salt was a staple in food, his income could rival the salaries of the highest-ranking officials at court.

"So... tempting..." he slurred. "Such... a pity... to be in the whorehouse... why don't you come with me?"

The courtesan kept her head down. Pieces of jade dangling from her hairpins swayed lightly. It was difficult to gauge if she were frightened or shy.

Chu burped, spread his arms, and lunged forward.

She moved—not fast, yet deft enough to miss his arms by a hair's breadth. Chu's sleeve brushed past her shoulder as he pitched forward and almost ended up leaning half of his body out of the boat.

He shook his head and let out a hiccup. Seeing that she made to leave, he reached out to her again,

2

this time determined that she should not evade his embrace.

She ducked. For a second, her gossamer sash, like a yellow mist, fluttered before his face and he caught a whiff of her perfume. Yet why couldn't he touch her? His arms met air and he lost his balance, tumbling on the floor.

The courtesan was still holding the lute, looking down at him.

"Mr. Chu, I am afraid you had too much to drink," she said sweetly.

"Nonsense!" he blurted, trying to get up.

She extended her hand, caught the folds of his long sleeves, and helped him up.

"Is it true," she breathed near his ear, "that the wife of the bricklayer Dong-Fong is at your residence?"

She was so near, so tempting… Chu didn't even think.

"Yes, but…"

"You're tired," she interrupted, and her fingers brushed lightly across his shoulder blades. "Please allow me to assist you to rest."

She smelled of peach blossoms and wine. Chu tried to grope her—how slender and shapely her waist looked! But for some dastardly reason, he couldn't lift his arms. He couldn't touch her. Had the wine numbed his senses?

The courtesan had her arm around his waist, half-carrying him toward the rooms built on the boat. It was obvious what they were heading for. Except for a few envious glances, most could only sigh and wish they made as much as Chu did.

Near dawn, a boat man was up and preparing for the day. His job was to escort people across the river, and though it was still ridiculously early, there were people who needed a ride, especially those who were arriving from another town.

There was something wrong with the waters. Something large—too large to be a duck, yet too small to be a raft—was floating on the river. The unknown object drifted nearer. It was a human body, the skin bluish and purplish and coming off the flesh.

"Aaargh!"

Soon, the word spread like fire through Yangzhou city. Chu Tou, the affluent salt merchant whose personal assets rivalled aristocrats, and who was known for luring and abducting young women into his household, had somehow lost his balance in a bout of heavy drinking and fallen into the river.

All was quiet at the compound of Governor Shue Song except for an owl suddenly taking off from a large oak tree.

The owl, however, did not fly away from a mere impulse. A figure in a black cloak had darted to the tree, which was leaning against the high wall around the compound, and swiftly climbed up and hid in the leafy branches. Making sure that no one was in the back yard, the black-clad figure hoisted herself onto the wall and jumped down. She landed on the ground as lightly as though she were a cat.

In a flash, she reached the servants' quarters, which were located in the northeast corner of the back yard. There was a small door in the high wall, convenient for the servants to pass through when they came back with purchases, but of course it was locked and barred during the night.

At the very end of the servants' quarters, right next to the storage shed, was her own room. She didn't even consider entering through the door—it was locked as well. She merely pushed up the shutters and leaped in through the window.

It was nearing dawn by now; though it was still dark, through the narrow opening she had left in her window, she could make out the furnishings of her room. She took off a bundle she had been carrying on her back and stashed it under her bed. It contained the fine clothes and ornaments she had worn just a few hours earlier. She liked the lute she had used, but it was too bulky to carry around. Besides, it belonged to the whorehouse.

The girl held up a round bronze mirror and started to remove her makeup. In her haste to return home, much of the powder and rouge was smeared and smudged. But it was of small consequence; she had accomplished her mission.

She soaked a wad of cotton in water and dabbed at her face, rinsing off the powder and lipstick. With makeup, she was beautiful and alluring, like a painted doll. Now, with her face clean and her hair free of ornaments, she still looked pretty, but by no means would she stand out in a crowd. Her eyes were of a perfect almond shape, but she lacked a crease in her eyelids, which made her look plain. She had an attractive heart-shaped face with a small mouth, but her nose was too flat. Her complexion was all right— her skin was smooth and white, but it didn't possess a shell-pink hue like some of her peers'. She had to rely on rouge for a glowing skin.

It didn't matter, anyway. One didn't need to be good-looking to excel in her job. Acute eyesight and sharp hearing were more important. Still, it helped when one had to disguise as a courtesan.

She made a mess of her things in the room, and climbed into bed. In a distance, a rooster crowed.

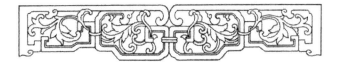

2

The sound of hooves clattered over cobbled stones as the third son of Governor Shue returned home. Fang was a young man around twenty, tall and broad-shouldered and bronze-skinned. A handsome fellow, with eyes the colour of ripe blackberries, high cheekbones, and a strong, aristocratic chin, he turned many a girl's head when he rode by. He wore a long, flowing red cape, an expensive black leather belt, and boots of deer hide. He looked just everything a young man of privilege should be—well-groomed, virile, and confident. Another young man followed him, also similarly attired in hunting clothes.

"Young Master!" A servant rushed from the stables to take the horse. "How was the expedition?"

"Several hares, two wild pheasants, and a mountain deer. We'll be having a feast tonight."

"Your father will be pleased to hear it."

Fang grinned. Turning to the young man behind him, he asked, "Chow, you're joining us for tonight?"

The man shook his head and tossed a large sack of game at him. "You're welcome to my share."

"Ah, you're in a hurry to be home?" There was a mischievous gleam in Fang's eyes. "Can't wait to see Opal? One whole year and you're still like glue together?"

"Quit it." Chow pretended to swipe at him, though a blush spread over his face, right down to his neck. "Rather than making fun of a married man, why don't you concentrate your energy on wooing *your* girl, instead? Last time I've heard, you didn't even have the gumption to present her a gift."

"You know she isn't the type to be swayed by expensive gifts," Fang said, though his jubilant mood waned slightly. "But I have plans. Just wait and see."

"I'll look forward to the wedding day," Chow said with a smile.

"Me too!" the servant, who was still standing nearby, echoed.

With a glare at both men, Fang removed his cape and handed over the reins. "I need a bath. Tell the servants to draw up hot water immediately."

"Right away, Young Master!"

When Fang emerged from his bath, all spruce and clean, he called for Shu-Mo, a manservant who was only a few years his junior. Shu-Mo had worked in the household since he was a child and had practically grown up with him. Sometimes they were more like friends than master and servant.

"I need your opinion." Fang held up a jade belt hook and a gold pendant. "Which one do you think looks better on me?"

Shu-Mo couldn't help chuckling. Fang, usually so confident and assured, was actually looking nervous, and Shu-Mo knew the reason why.

"I believe jade is more—er—sophisticated, Young Master," he replied with a grin. "It's what Master Shue himself usually wears."

Fang considered a moment. "Yes, I think you're right." He fastened the hook on his belt and ran a hand through his hair. "Do I look all right?"

"Oh, surely you'd rather hear it from the lady than me." Shu-Mo winked. "All right, our Young Master is positively ravishing." Then, with a touch of reluctance, he added, "At least several maidservants I know are eager to gain your attention. Silver Peony begged me the other day to have the privilege of changing your bedsheets and sweeping the floor of your room."

Fang grinned, but soon his shoulders slumped. He knew he was good-looking, but it was hard to tell if the girl he wanted to impress would be drawn by his looks alone. He highly doubted it; they had lived under the same roof for ten years, yet she never giggled, batted her eyelashes, or pretended to drop her handkerchief when she was around him.

"Well, send for Hong now. Tell her that I want to hear her play the song that she performed at Eldest Brother's wedding feast."

When Shu-Mo hurried away, Fang dropped in a chair and tried to think of what to say when she arrived. Then he shook his head and laughed. It was absurd, him being worried about how a maidservant should see him.

But then she was no ordinary maid. Hong had come from a noble family, but her father had lost favour with the emperor and been thrown into prison. His compound and possessions had been confiscated, and Hong and her mother had been sold as slaves. Were it not for the compassion of his father, Governor Shue, it was likely that they would have ended up in a brothel.

He didn't know how long he had been drawn to her. It seemed strange, since there were so many pretty maids in the house, and considering his looks and status, he could pick anyone, or several. A couple of his brothers did just that—taking several concubines in addition to one wife, and still frequenting the brothel. Hong didn't stand out either—Golden Lotus was prettier, Silver Peony was more solicitous, but something inexplicable about Hong attracted him.

Fang cast his gaze over the garden outside. There was a magnificent pine tree just a few paces from his room, stretching over a small pond with pink lotus flowers floating on the still waters. Eleven years ago, he had been first introduced to Hong, right under this tree. His nanny had been friends with Hong's mother, who had occasionally paid a visit to the governor's house.

He could still remember seven-year-old Hong, with round pink cheeks and pink ribbons in her black hair, peering shyly at him behind her mother. He remembered how his nanny, Nurse Chang, had taken his hand and told him to "be nice to the little sister and show her around."

He remembered their first game: playing hide-and-seek in the garden. He had turned his back against her as he leaned into the pine tree and counted from one to twenty. He remembered she had wanted to catch the yellow butterflies hovering near the peony bushes, and he had asked for a net. He remembered sharing a big ripe pear with her, simply because neither of them could finish the pear on their own.

They had only played together a few times, but he had always looked forward to her visits.

However, everything had changed when Hong's father was persecuted.

Fang never forgot the day when his father had taken him for a walk, and right in the city centre was a display of slaves for sale. He noticed Hong right away—even though her clothes were dirty and tattered, her skin smudged with dirt, her hair bushy and unkempt.

When she had entered the Shue household, still a child of eight, she was quiet and reserved. She never complained or demanded special treatment. Sometimes he would hide and watch her practise the lute. He loved the serene, calm expression she wore, and the lovely music that seemed to flow from her heart, not just from her fingers.

But he was clueless on how to approach her. Although Hong was technically a servant, she had gained favour in his father's eyes. Shue Song allowed her to transcribe and sort books for him, and treated her well. When an elderly relative demanded to buy Hong, Shue had tactfully refused. He would not have Hong removed if she was unwilling.

Which was why even Fang, the governor's son, who could have any maid in his service, could not simply order Hong to come to him. Not that he would force any maid to be his concubine, anyway.

Shue had long ago taught him that he should never abuse his power as one of the masters in the house.

Fang sighed. In a way, he preferred to court Hong, like the heroes in the romances he read. But Hong treated him just the same as everyone else. She was reserved, polite, and respectful around him— which only made things more frustrating. He didn't know what he could do to make her notice him, to realise that he was not simply a childhood friend. He wanted to make her his, keep her by his side, rather than seeing her serve his family and allowing them a share in her attentions. It was time to do something.

When Shu-Mo returned, Fang sat up. "Where is she?"

"She said she was feeling unwell." Shu-Mo looked sorry for his young master. "She begs that you excuse her today, but should you require another time, she would be happy to be of service."

"Is it serious?" Fang demanded. "Has a physician been sent for her?"

"No, she said it was just a cold. It isn't a big deal, but she doesn't want Young Master to be infected."

"I see." Fang slumped back in his chair.

Great. Just when he got up the nerve to request her to play, something that normally only his father commanded, she happened to fall ill.

"It's not that she refused you." Shu-Mo tried to comfort him. "She promised to play another time."

Fang scowled. "Be off and leave me be."

Still, when the door closed behind him, Fang did feel that he had to make an extra effort. There was talk of his father taking Hong for a mistress, now that she was eighteen and of marriageable age. From what he could observe, Shue Song did treat Hong differently, but Fang was certain that if Hong was unwilling, his father would not force her. If only he could make her notice him soon…

Fang called another maid. "Golden Lotus? Have a bowl of chicken broth sent to Hong."

In her room, Hong turned over and adjusted her position on the wooden pillow. She had only slept for two hours last night. Worried that everyone would see the dark circles under her eyes, not to mention that her back ached horribly from the mad ride overnight, she decided to feign illness. It wasn't too hard—she pulled strands of hair over her face and pitched her voice low. She wasn't looking too well anyway, from a serious lack of sleep and a huge expenditure of energy.

She put a hand on her forehead, thinking. Just a while ago, Shu-Mo had rapped on her door, telling her that the young master wanted her attention. She had faked a throaty voice and told him she was sick. It had worked this time, but she couldn't go on pretending she was sick every time she made a nightly excursion.

It had been easier when the victims lived in the vicinity of the district, but Yangzhou City had taken three hours on horseback. She had tried to finish the job as quickly as possible, but even though disposing of Chu had been simple enough, she was exhausted after riding nonstop, sneaking in the city past curfew, and making her way to the governor's compound.

"Why don't you leave the Shues?" her *sifu* had asked. "You have worked for the governor for ten years. You have paid your dues long ago."

But she was reluctant to leave—yet. As much as she wanted to help her *sifu* eliminate crooks, she was used to living in the Shue household. She was grateful for the governor's lenient treatment, and she would like to stay for some time, until she could be certain that there would be no regrets when she left.

Footsteps echoed outside. Another knock on the door.

"Hong, it's me! I've brought something for your cold." It was Golden Lotus, one of the maidservants.

Hong immediately pulled the blankets up to her chin. "Come in," she said, in what she hoped was a croaky voice.

Golden Lotus entered, carrying a ceramic pot on a wooden tray. She was one of the prettiest maids in the household—a plump young girl barely sixteen, with skin that resembled roses and cream, large eyes that usually sparkled with spirit, and a pretty laugh that made people think of spring.

"Here, sister." She set the pot on the table. A savoury smell of onions and garlic wafted in the air. "Come and have some chicken broth."

"Thank you." Hong faked a cough. "It's very sweet of you to make it for me."

Golden Lotus grinned. "Young Master ordered us to cook for you. In fact, he even supervised us! He stood there the whole time when we did the boning and selected the herbs, and he even did most of the boiling and stirring. Honestly"—Golden Lotus suddenly became very severe—"you should consider yourself fortunate, Hong. I haven't heard of any young lords who are willing to cook for a woman, much less a maid."

14

Hong kept her face down. She had had some inkling that the young master fancied her, but she hadn't expected that he would go to the lengths of invading the kitchen.

"That is very kind of him. Please tell him I am very grateful for his consideration." She forgot to fake her voice this time, but Golden Lotus didn't notice.

"Here's a better idea: why don't you go to his rooms once you're better? He will be delighted to see you. I can lend you a second-hand robe that Miss Lynn gave me the other day. It's low-cut here"—she drew a finger across her bosom—"but don't worry, it's not too revealing. I'd say it's much better than the dreary blue robe you wear every day. Honestly, you should wear brighter colours—how about a nice crimson red? Since your name means red anyway."

Hong smiled, but shook her head. She *did* know how to dress up—the fancy, ornate dress she had worn the night before easily outshone any of Golden Lotus's—but she preferred to keep a low profile at the governor's house. Plus, after years of training with her *sifu*, who led a frugal life, Hong was used to living simply.

"I can't. I promised Master Liu that I would visit him."

"Old Man Liu?" Golden Lotus wrinkled her pretty little nose. "I know he's famous and all, but seriously, you've been taking lessons from him for ten years. Surely you don't need to go and see him so frequently. It isn't as if he lacks company, he doesn't even want to live with his grandsons."

"He is my mentor," Hong said sharply. "Do not speak condescendingly of him."

Golden Lotus was rather taken aback by her tone. Usually Hong was calm and soft-spoken. Rarely did she display any temper.

"Fine." Golden Lotus shrugged, heading for the door. "If you'd prefer the company of an old man when you could be seeing our dashing young master, it's your choice."

The door closed behind her with a bang.

Hong looked down at the bowl of broth. Steam was still rising from it. Slowly, she got off the bed and reached the table. Taking a wooden spoon, she ladled a bit of hot soup and tasted it.

The broth was slightly saltier than she liked, but then she preferred her food simple and bland. Nevertheless, Hong smiled as she finished the bowl.

3

The next day, Hong prepared to visit her *sifu*. Unlike the sophisticated process she went through when disguising herself as a courtesan, she slipped into a simple dark blue cotton robe and selected a snowy white girdle. Then she dabbed a small amount of face powder over her face, twisted her long black hair into a chignon on top of her head and secured it with a hairpin of carved ebony.

Time to begin her daily routine of tidying and preparing her master's office.

Governor Shue's office was situated in the main building. From the servants' quarters, one had to pass through the rear garden by one of the many winding paths, go past pavilions, ponds, and various shrubbery, reach the rear buildings, which were the living quarters of womenfolk, and finally arrive at the main hall. It was much easier for guests entering from the front gates—they just had to pass through the front courtyard.

It was quiet in the main compound. The Shue family was still having breakfast in the east side building; she could see several servants, Golden Lotus included, hurrying between the side building and the kitchen, carrying trays of rice and large jars of soy milk.

Only a few elderly servants were dusting the furniture in the grand parlour. Hong greeted them with a friendly "Good morning," and entered the governor's office.

She scrubbed the floor, polished the porcelain vases, refilled the lamps with hemp oil, dusted the bookshelf, and set out the brushes, ink, and paper on the mahogany desk.

Just when she finished grinding the inkstone, Shue Song entered the room. He was a tall, distinguished-looking man with a well-trimmed beard and pleasant features. Although he was nearing fifty, Shue looked young for his age; the strenuous military exercise that he still undertook daily made him look fitter than most of his peers, who had taken up a life of luxury and debauchery.

"Good morning, Master." Hong dipped into a curtsy.

"As punctual as usual, Hong, dear." Shue smiled at her. "I heard from Fang that you were unwell yesterday?"

"Yes. But I am much better now, Master."

Shue strode to the desk and sat down, leaning his elbow against the armrest.

"The weather being mercurial lately, do take care of yourself," he said, then lowered his voice. "It has been a year, no?"

Hong nodded. "Master, do not worry. I *chose* this path. I do not regret it."

Shue regarded her pensively. Although she was technically a servant, she had been of a well-to-do family, and she could have simply married into the Shue family—thus ensuring a normal, secure, prosperous life forever. She was no beauty, but he was certain that someone among the servants would be happy to take her as a bride—not to mention his third son, who seemed to be much taken with her since they were children. Yet since she had revealed to him that she was training to be a vigilante, he had had the feeling that it would not be long before she left the household.

A vigilante did not associate with government officials. A vigilante usually evaded or broke the law. Hong did not want her secret identity to inconvenience her master, even though he knew she was doing it for a good cause.

Sometimes he regretted that he had allowed her to continue training with Old Man Liu, that he had allowed his friend's only daughter to undertake such a perilous profession, but it was too late.

"Master? If you do not need my services later, I should like to request leave to visit my *sifu* today. I have been neglecting my music studies lately."

Shue understood. She was to give Old Man Liu a report of her mission the day before.

"By all means," he said, taking up his brush. "Please pass along my regards. You will be back for dinner?"

"Yes." Then, as though touched by remorse, Hong bowed again. "Thank you, Master. I will return as soon as I can."

Once she was finished with her morning duties, Hong hurried back to her room. By now, the family had finished breakfast, and the servants had cleared things away. A lot more activity was going on. Several girls, all dressed in bright colours of crimson, yellow, and green, were playing football in the garden, right by a golden pavilion.

While football was popular in the military and often used as a means of leisurely training, it was enjoyed by womenfolk as well. Rules were simple— there was no limit on the number of people, nor restrictions on which parts of the body might touch the ball. All it required was that the ball must not fall on the ground. The person who failed to catch the ball was labelled the loser—and usually punished by drinking a concoction of lemon juice mixed with peppers.

A gasp rose from the girls. One of them had kicked too exuberantly—the leather ball sailed over the pavilion, hit the green-glazed tiles, and rolled off the roof, landing near Hong's feet.

Hong was tempted to send the ball flying back to them with a well-aimed kick, but she always tried to conceal her martial abilities as much as possible. It was easier if people took her to be a quiet type who just played the lute and transcribed notes for the governor.

So she just picked up the ball and threw it back, deliberately making it a lousy throw. It sailed beyond the pavilion and would have landed in a clump of azaleas, had not a girl darted forward and caught the ball deftly with one hand.

It was Shue's only daughter, Lynn. She was a pretty, vivacious girl just past seventeen. Though she was still young, she excelled in football, often participating in games with her brothers. Hong had served her occasionally, bringing her snacks and sewing her clothes. Despite that Lynn was sometimes rather vain and self-centred, being the only girl in the family, Hong liked the young mistress's straightforward manner and knew she had a good heart.

"What're you standing there for?" Lynn called. "Come join us!"

"Sorry, but not today. I must be seeing Master Liu."

"Aww, come on, Hong! Just a game!"

Hong smiled, but shook her head. "I'm already late. Please enjoy yourselves."

It was a cool, breezy day in the city. Making sure that the bag containing her lute was securely strapped on her back, Hong proceeded to walk from the governor's compound to the east gate of the city. She could have borrowed a donkey from the stables, but she preferred walking as one way to exercise. Besides, the roads could get extremely crowded.

The city had changed much since she had first come here as a slave. Since there had been no war here, the city was now a prosperous urban centre. Elms and pagodas lined the streets, shops of all sizes populated the market, the monastery and temples were beautifully maintained, most of the people appeared to be neatly dressed and did not lack for food.

Of course, the shady areas still existed—the brothels and gambling rings thrived with patrons. She still saw beggars and disabled people crouching by the road sometimes, knocking their foreheads on the mud. But it was a much better world than the one she remembered in her childhood, and she was working hard to ensure that it stayed that way.

"Have some pity, miss?" A beggar raised his head, showing a mouthful of yellowed broken teeth. "Some alms to spare?"

"Not at the present, I'm afraid," Hong whispered, bending close to him. Were the maids at the Shue household to see her now, they would be appalled at the sight of Hong, meticulously dressed and arrayed, conversing at such close proximity with a filthy beggar. "But I will let you know when the time comes."

She straightened up and walked slowly away. Her exchange with the beggar seemed harmless enough, but in fact, her *sifu* maintained a network of beggar spies—usually disabled people—throughout the city and beyond. Because he himself was disabled, her *sifu* chose to seek those who were blind, deaf, or missing a limb, and told them that in return for information on crooks and criminals, he would supply them a fair number of coppers. The beggars were useful especially for finding out information, as normally people wouldn't pay attention to them.

She felt someone tug on her sleeve. It was Ah-Ming, a child of ten. His mother had died early and now it was only his father and his grandmother living together. Ah-Ming also worked as an assistant at her friend Meng-Ting's drugstore, where he could learn a new trade and also earn a bit to help out his family.

"This is for you," Ah-Ming said shyly. He held out a bunch of daisies. "From my grandmother's garden."

"Why, thank you," Hong smiled, pinning the flowers on her sash. "So you're not working at Meng-Ting's today?"

Ah-Ming shook his head. "He told me to take the day off."

"Hello, Miss Hong!" a hearty voice said. It was Ah-Ming's father, a stout, middle-aged man. "Come and have a bowl of noodle soup, it's on me!"

"Thank you, but I have to be going."

"Pshaw, it won't take long! You're all skin and bones! How are you going to find a husband, hey?" At the time, being plump was considered attractive— it showed that the girl was well-fed and healthy.

"Please, Miss Hong," Ah-Ming said.

Unable to refuse their hospitality, Hong sat down at the little shop. Little did she know that this would be the last meal she ate there.

4

Old Man Liu lived in a secluded compound right outside the city. He was a blind old man around seventy years old, and was known to be an eccentric person of a volatile temper. Few found favour in his eyes. Yet he was still highly respected due to his proficiency in music; it was rumoured that he had trained in the emperor's palace when he was young, but the war had ravaged the capital and taken his eyesight. He had two grandsons, but unlike most elderly people, he chose not to live with his family. Instead, he preferred to spend his days with his mahogany lute and bamboo flute.

Hong was one of the few people who had managed to form a friendship with Liu. Nine years ago, she had happened to meet him near a temple and he had offered to teach her the lute. Since then, Hong had travelled to his compound every ten days, taking music lessons from him. As a result, her music ability surpassed all servants in Shue's household and her performance had been in great demand any time there was a feast or ceremony. But it wasn't just music lessons that Liu had taught her. It was the martial arts that had changed her life completely.

When she left the city through the east gate, it was another hour on foot before she arrived at Old Man Liu's residence, a medium-sized compound that was at least two hundred years old. It stood at the foot of a hill that was covered by bamboos. Due to the remoteness of Liu's residence, few people would pass by this area, apart from occasional visits from Hong and Liu's grandsons. Some said that Liu preferred it this way—it was rare that an old blind man of seventy would choose to live alone when clearly he had offspring to care for him, but then he was always an eccentric old man.

The wooden door swung open before Hong had raised her hand to knock. A young man in his early twenties looked out. He was neatly dressed in a grey cotton robe and wore a white gauze cap. He smelled of ginseng and rhubarb.

"You're a bit late today," he said. "Come in quickly, Grandpa has been waiting."

"I had a snack at Ah-Ming's father's shop." Hong stepped through the doorway. "*Sifu*'s hearing is as good as ever, Meng-Ting."

"Tell me about it." Meng-Ting shook his head. "You can *never* sneak up on him. I swear he can hear how many acupuncture needles I drop on the ground by accident."

They entered a small courtyard, which was quite bare except for a bamboo couch and an accompanying armrest set in a corner. A hunchbacked elderly man with grey whiskers sat cross-legged on the couch, a wooden bowl filled with dried melon seeds set upon the armrest.

Once Hong stepped into the courtyard, the elderly man grabbed a handful of seeds and threw them at Hong. The girl immediately spread out her arms; in a few swift, fluid motions, she caught the seeds in her hands. Not a single one hit her face or body, or worse, the ground.

"Typical welcome," Meng-Ting muttered.

Hong came to the old man's side and laid the seeds on the armrest.

"*Sifu*, I have come."

"Hmm." Old Man Liu popped a melon seed in his mouth. "Not one seed on the ground. I should have used a larger amount."

"Did everything go well with the salt merchant, Hong?" Meng-Ting asked.

Hong gave an account of her mission. She had sneaked into the house of a former prostitute who rented out clothes, grabbed a set of fine robes and matching accessories, and left a big piece of gold on the table. Then she had slipped in the brothel next door, found an empty room and got dressed. Arrayed like a normal courtesan, she had pretended that she was a newcomer and asked a servant which boat was engaged for Merchant Chu that night. The rest was simple. Her lute performance had easily attracted an audience.

"But you don't know how to swim!" Meng-Ting said.

"Many people in the city can't swim either," Hong said. "Besides, the boats for nightly entertainment were huge and had entire rooms built on them."

Old Man Liu grunted. "There's not much danger for Hong when she's dealing with an old lecherous merchant. I'm more concerned about the time she needed to accomplish the mission. What if her next mission takes her to the capital?"

"She'll have to leave, sooner or later," Meng-Ting said. "Aren't you planning to take leave of the governor soon?"

Hong felt a pang in her heart, but she kept her expression neutral.

"Yes. I am looking for an opportunity."

"At any rate, we'd better continue working on your martial skills." Liu slowly got up from the bamboo couch. "Let's go to the training room. Meng-Ting, I want another pot of tea. Be sure not to over-steep the tea leaves."

"I never over-steep," Meng-Ting protested. He was a physician, for God's sake. He was an expert in brewing herbal remedies that required meticulous attention; there was no way he could mess up boiling a simple cup of tea.

Liu hobbled towards the building, and Hong followed him. She did not assist him, as Liu was already too familiar with the surroundings and moved around as though his eyesight was perfectly normal.

Liu led the way to an inner room which had no windows and motioned Hong to close the door. It was completely dark except for the faint light filtering in from under the slit of the door. However, Hong's well-trained eyes detected a narrow table with a dozen candles on it. They were arranged in a rather haphazard manner—some of them were close together, while others were set far apart.

"Go to that corner." Liu pointed with a long bony finger. "Get out your darts, girlie, and be prepared."

Slowly but steadily, the elderly man lit a fire by using a tinder box that was also lying on the table, and started lighting the candles. Hong waited silently, but she wasn't idle. Her gaze swept over the table as she counted the number of candles and reached inside her robes to take out the same number of darts.

"Now let's see how many tries you need today," Liu said, when he finished lighting the last one. "Remember, your sole purpose is to extinguish the flame only. Woe be with you if you knock down a single candle."

"Yes, *sifu*." Hong flexed the darts between her fingers. There was a draught coming from the slit below the door, and the candle flames flickered eerily in the darkness. A slightly unpleasant smell from the candles burning, combined with the muskiness of the room, made her breathe rather uncomfortably.

Carefully, she took aim and released her darts. There were tiny sounds of the darts whipping through the air and sounds of poofs as the candles were extinguished one by one.

Liu, his brow furrowed, listened attentively.

"Eleven down," he announced. "Almost all. That's better than last time."

Hong bowed her head. The tone of his voice was not demanding, but it carried a note of criticism. She should have done better.

Liu moved towards the candles. Instead of rekindling them immediately, he started to break off the ends of some of them, so the dozen candles had different lengths. Then he rearranged their positions on the table. Finally, he took up the tinder box and rekindled every single candle.

"Here," he said gruffly. "Now you've almost perfected extinguishing candles of the same size, let's see how you fare with them in different lengths."

"Yes, *sifu*."

The training session carried on accordingly, with Liu continuously rearranging the candles' positions; when Hong managed to extinguish them all in one single aim, he again changed tactics. When Meng-Ting came in with the tea, Liu made him bring extra tables and benches and chairs.

"Go outside," he ordered, once Meng-Ting had brought in enough furniture.

Meng-Ting wiped the sweat from his brow and prepared to leave, but Liu stopped him.

"I meant *her*," he snapped. "Don't want her memorising the candles' locations while we work. I want Hong to take aim at the candles as soon as she sees them. We need to hone her ability to react immediately and efficiently."

A few minutes later, Meng-Ting came out. Hong was standing silently near the door, looking up at the sky.

"You're to go in now," he said. Then he lowered his voice to a whisper. "Glad that it's you he chose to be your disciple, not me. Don't think I could survive a session like this."

Hong smiled but said nothing. Perhaps she did have some natural talent, but she knew well that Old Man Liu had chosen her because she was an orphan without attachments. A vigilante could not be ruthless when he had close family and relatives to think of. Furthermore, since she did not lack material comfort while living at Shue's house, she would not be easily swayed by huge bounties. She would remain loyal. And since she also knew what it was like to be poor and defenceless, during the year that her father had lost favour and been sentenced to prison, she would have more compassion and incentive to rid corruption, right wrongs, and assist the weak.

Meng-Ting, who had expressed an interest in having at least five children, would not be as good a choice as her. Besides, he was well suited in his profession as a highly-skilled physician.

She readied her darts and opened the door.

Two hours later, Hong's arms were aching and her fingers were red and bruised. She did not make a word of complaint; unlike Meng-Ting, she never raised dissent in front of a senior.

Old Man Liu told her she could have a break.

"Your aim is all right," he pronounced. For Liu, "all right" equalled "spectacular." "But your stamina is terrible. I should have made you carry more weights when you were a child, but you spend too much time at the governor's. Your skills may be good, but what use will they be if you run out of energy?"

"I am sorry." Hong looked on the floor, which was littered with darts. "I will strive to better my skills next time."

"If only there's some way…" Liu mused, and suddenly he straightened. "Someone is coming this way."

Hong dropped to the ground and listened carefully. Very faintly, she could hear the quick, firm tread of a person, who slowed down as he approached.

Whoever it was, she could not be caught practising in the training room.

"It doesn't seem to be Meng-Chou," Liu said, frowning. His hearing was superior in that he needn't press his ear to the ground, plus he was able to detect the difference in footfalls. Hong wondered when she could reach his level of hearing.

"My lute is outside," she said, indicating that they should pretend that they were in the middle of a music lesson.

Liu nodded. "Who on earth could it be?"

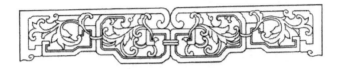

5

Fang walked briskly through the streets of the city, feeling slightly irritated. He had gone to his father earlier, asking for Hong, but learnt she had gone to Old Man Liu's. Wasn't it just a week ago that she had visited the old man? It seemed that she preferred her music instructor's company more than being at the governor's.

Since he was not taking his steed today, Fang decided to take a shortcut. He rounded a corner, entering an alley, and to his surprise, saw the magistrate's son, Ho Jiang-Min, with a young woman. It was Opal, the wife of his friend Chow. She had worked previously for the magistrate's daughter before she got married.

Jiang-Min had backed Opal against a wall, one arm blocking her from running into the main street.

"My, my, my," the magistrate's son drawled. "Marriage has made you even prettier, Opal. How rosy your cheek looks." He reached out to stroke her face, but she turned her head, trying to evade his touch.

"Ma… master. Please don't…"

"Excuse me," Fang said sharply. "Get away from her."

Instantly, the young woman gave a little cry of relief and ran towards Fang.

Jiang-Min's eyes blazed. "Why, isn't it Little Mr. Shue, the *youngest* of the governor's sons. Trying to play the hero, huh? But in case you didn't know, this woman was in my household. I was her first, not her husband."

"Stop!" Opal screamed. "Stop saying that!"

"Why, it's the truth. So why do you even care about being faithful to your husband now, huh? There's nothing he saw that I haven't seen on you—"

Splash. Fang had seized his collar and tossed him over his shoulder. Jiang-Min went flying in the air and landed in a large puddle, his face deep in the muddy water.

Had Jiang-Min trained in fighting, he might have defended himself better against the son of a military governor, but he was the typical rich young man who preferred idle pursuits that required little physical effort. He was more into watching people (and animals) fight than undertaking fighting lessons himself.

"How dare you!" he spluttered. "You wait until I tell my father—"

"Go ahead." Fang folded his arms. "Let him know that you are picking on a maid who is already married. Let him know how useless you are." He cast a contemptuous look over Jiang-Min's mud-splattered robes.

Jiang-Min glared—though with his face completely covered in mud, he didn't look the least intimidating.

"I'm warning you, Fang, this time you might have the upper hand, but next time you won't be so lucky! I'll never forget how you insulted me."

He stalked away, the end of his robes leaving a muddy trail behind him.

Fang looked at his retreating back, feeling disgusted. His elder brothers had married and taken concubines, but they would never touch a married woman, not to mention humiliate her in front of another man. Really, how much lower could the magistrate's son get?

"Thank you, Master Fang." Opal bowed to him.

"Better avoid being caught alone with him," Fang said. As a matter of fact, he thought that Opal shouldn't be walking alone in a deserted alley. She was really pretty—heart-shaped face, doe eyes, rosebud mouth. "Where are you going? I can walk with you to your destination."

"No!" Opal blurted, then checked herself. Was that a flicker of fear in her eyes? "Um, I was going to the winehouse, but you don't have to. It's very near."

"At least let me accompany you to a street where there are more people," Fang said firmly. "You ought to avoid places like this."

Opal relented. Fang walked her to the main street.

"Did the magistrate's son bother you before?"

Opal shook her head. "It was just bad luck I saw him today."

"It's easier to take the shortcut, but honestly, you should watch out for yourself. Chow can't be with you all the time, you know?"

Opal flushed. Fang wondered if he should tell Chow about the magistrate's son; no man could tolerate his wife being molested, not to mention in broad daylight! But then he decided that he should keep quiet. It should be Opal doing the telling.

When they reached the main street, Opal bowed. "Thank you, Master Fang. I can go on by myself." And she left abruptly, as though she were afraid of being seen with him. Fang was puzzled for a while. Of the few times he had dined at Chow's place, Opal had seemed quite friendly and cordial. It wasn't as if they were holding hands or doing anything inappropriate—why did she have the urge to be rid of him so quickly?

Little did he know that his brief meeting with Opal would eventually bring him much trouble.

After parting with Opal, Fang quickened his pace towards Old Man Liu's place, which was taking some time to locate. He had visited once or twice before, but he still could not get used to how remote the place was. It was understandable why Hong did not mind trekking halfway through the city to visit Liu; Fang knew that she preferred peace and quiet.

Fang lifted a hand and used the brass ring to knock on the door. To his surprise, it was Liu Meng-Ting, Liu's grandson and also a well-known physician in the city, who answered the door.

"Hello," Fang said, wondering why Meng-Ting was here. From what he had heard, Old Man Liu preferred to be left alone. "I am Governor Shue's third son—Fang is my name. I have a message to deliver from my father."

"Honoured to make your acquaintance," Meng-Ting said with a smile. "No wonder your face seems familiar; I was summoned to the governor's residence just a couple months ago to treat a servant's illness. Please come in, if you'll excuse my grandfather's austere living quarters."

Inside the courtyard, Old Man Liu sat on a bamboo couch, tapping the couch with his forefinger. Hong was sitting directly across him on a low wooden stool, strumming on her lute. In the tranquillity, the music from her lute flowed through the air like honey and nectar.

Meng-Ting moved towards them, but Fang detained him. "Let her finish the song," he whispered.

Meng-Ting looked surprised, but nodded.

When the last note died away on the lute, Fang stepped forward. "Master Liu." He made a short bow, even though he knew the old man couldn't see him. "Shue Fang begs your pardon for his sudden intrusion. My father, the governor, has sent me personally."

Liu raised his eyebrows, but said gruffly, "Flattered, young man. How can I be of assistance to the governor?"

Fang held out a red visiting card hesitantly, wondering if he should give it to Liu or Meng-Ting. He decided to speak first.

"My father's fiftieth birthday is in two weeks. We have planned a grand celebration for him, and it would be a great honour if Master Liu could make an appearance and grace the guests with his music."

"That is very kind, but I must decline," Liu said. "At my age, my frailty deems it unfit to be in the jostle and bustle of company. And my fingers have grown rusty; my performance is not as it has been. However, tell your father that I shall teach Hong a new song that she may perform in my place."

Fang glanced at Hong, who had risen when he arrived, and was standing quietly with a serene expression. When Liu finished speaking, she gave him a small smile that made his heart jump.

"I shall do my best." She bowed her head.

Liu grunted. "Well, that's settled, then. Go home, girlie, you've been through enough today. Meanwhile, I'll think about what you should prepare for next time. Come back in five days."

"Yes, *sifu*."

It was a long walk back to the governor's residence, but Fang appreciated it. He had thought about using a horse, but then decided against it. He had been hunting the day before and wanted to let his horse have a good rest. Plus, a walk in the city and to the outskirts would be good exercise. And now, with Hong walking by his side, his spirits soared. It wasn't often that the two of them could be alone together. Too many siblings and servants at the governor's compound.

"How… how are you feeling now?" he asked. "Your cold, I mean?"

"Much better. Thank you, Young Master, for the chicken broth."

"Oh, it wasn't anything," Fang said, though he couldn't help grinning. "I don't—we don't want you falling sick. By the way," he took a deep breath, "since you are fully recovered, would you come and play for me some time? You can also practise the song that you'll be playing on Father's birthday ceremony."

There was a slight blush on her cheeks, but she nodded.

"As you wish, Young Master."

Fang couldn't help feeling disappointed, even though she had given her consent. She was so maddeningly polite and respectful that he wanted to shake her. She was only saying yes because he was her master—or rather, one of her masters. If his brothers also ordered her to perform for them, she wouldn't (and couldn't) refuse, either. It was frustrating, really.

They rounded a corner to the main street.

A grand procession was making its way down the street. Everyone in the procession was dressed splendidly in red; even the sedan chair in the middle was decorated with red ribbons and tassels. Trumpets blared, flutes sang, and small bronze gongs clanged. Two women with red peonies in their hair were carrying baskets of candied fruit, which they threw to the onlookers who had gathered on the sides of the streets. Some children squealed with glee when they caught a handful of candy.

"How splendid!" someone in the audience was saying. "Which prosperous family is marrying off their daughter?"

"It's the magistrate's daughter," another said. "She just got engaged to Guo's eldest son a while ago."

"You mean that stupendously wealthy merchant Guo? A good choice, but I thought the magistrate would strive for someone who has a position in the palace. He was doing so well when his eldest daughter became the emperor's Grand Concubine."

"Times aren't the same as before. Don't you know that merchants can *buy* their titles now? It's plain hard cash that's of worth now! If I had a daughter, I would also rather she married a rich businessman than a poor official!"

Fang glanced at the bridegroom, a rather plump young man who sat complacently on a beautiful horse that looked to be imported from Central Asia. Not remotely handsome, but Fang hadn't heard that Guo Yen-Bin had any bad habits. Some young men of rich families had terrible reputations—frequenting brothels, gambling houses, winehouses, etc. Even Fang's two elder brothers occasionally indulged in "pleasure" respites.

Merchant Guo had made a fortune in the silk market and Guo Yen-Bin himself seemed a decent young man. Looked like the magistrate's daughter was not doing too badly, though her elder sister had done much better.

Fang had seen the magistrate's daughter, Ho Wen-Jun, several times before. His younger sister, Lynn, was a friend of Wen-Jun's. A stunningly beautiful girl, accomplished in poetry, music, and chess, but she didn't catch his fancy. She wasn't Hong.

As Fang noted the satisfied smirk of Guo Yen-Bin, his mind wandered off into a temporary fantasy. Perhaps one day he could also be astride a horse, wearing a red brocaded robe, leading his bride to his home. Then he sobered at the thought. Even if he managed to persuade Hong, according to customs, she could not be anything but a concubine. He would be expected to take a wife first, and intuition told him

39

that it would be a bad decision. Jealous wives who tortured concubines were not unusual. Fang did not fancy letting someone other than Hong share his bed, much less letting a jealous first wife mistreat her.

There was a light touch on his arm.

"Young Master?"

Belatedly, Fang realised that he had gone down the wrong alley. He was so lost in his own thoughts that he had not been conscious of the direction he was going.

"Are you all right?" she asked solicitously, her hand still on his arm. Her touch seemed to burn through him.

Fang swallowed. He knew she was only asking out of friendly concern, but still…

"Of course," he said, his voice sounding gruffer than it should be. "The noise… and there's so many people…" No, he shouldn't have yammered like that, he sounded like such a weakling.

Hong reached inside her long sleeves and produced a small silken pouch. She extracted a pill and handed it to him.

"Here, chew on this," she offered. "It's made of peppermint leaves. I sometimes take it when I'm tired."

Fang took the pill. A cool, refreshing taste spread through his mouth and went up his nose.

"Where did you get this?" he asked, smiling. "I might need some when Father gives me chores."

"Mr. Liu, the physician."

That young man who had come to answer the door? He felt a stab of jealousy.

"In that case, I should pester him for more the next time I see him," Fang finally said, hoping that he sounded natural. "Does he visit Old Man Liu's place often?"

"Occasionally."

Hong did not blush when she spoke of Liu Meng-Ting. Fang decided to put it aside; if she and Meng-Ting were together, they could have had plenty of chances. A tiny, evil part of him also whispered that a mere physician would stand no chance against him, considering their differences in station. But then, if his father decided to take Hong as a concubine, it would be a different playing game. He had to do something—and what better opportunity than the current moment?

Slowly, Fang reached out and enclosed her hand in his. Her skin was rough and callused—his heart contracted with a pang of affliction and sympathy. He knew that she willingly worked hard— both as a maidservant and a disciple—but he wished that she would learn to relax a bit in her busy life and to confide in him whenever she encountered trials.

The next second, she withdrew her hand—a move so light and fluid that it almost felt that her hand had vanished.

"I had better carry my lute," she said, without looking at him. "I'm afraid my bag isn't sturdy enough to keep it strapped on my back."

Was she embarrassed about holding hands in public, or was she simply averse to his touch? Fang kept his expression neutral, but inwardly he was hurt by her rejection. Perhaps he was being too hasty? He only hoped that her reason for snubbing him was not because she favoured another.

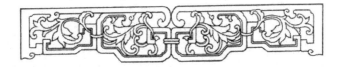

6

The next day, Hong had just finished dusting her master's room when Shue entered. He was a bit earlier than usual; she had not yet brought in his morning tea.

"Ah, good morning, Hong."

"Master," Hong respectfully replied, stepping aside so he could settle in his chair. "Would you like some tea? I can go to the kitchens right away."

"Not now. I have something important to discuss with you," Shue said, putting his elbows on the desk and looking at her. "I have been thinking for a while—you are turning nineteen next month, if I am correct?"

"Yes, master."

"I told you before that you will always have a home here. But Hong, my dear, it seems high time that you should have a family of your own. Have you not someone you fancy? If not, I can employ a reputable matchmaker. Rest assured that you will not marry someone without your consent."

Hong thought of Fang's flushed expression when she laid a hand on his arm, and his smile when he swallowed the peppermint pill. But she couldn't. Not when she was leading a double life. She had made an oath to her *sifu*, that in return for his training her, she would assist him in righting wrongs and eliminating evil. She had never regretted it, even if it meant sacrificing her chance to lead a normal life.

"It is very thoughtful of you, master," she said carefully. "But currently I am happy where I am. I have no wish to change." Her tone was respectful, but a quiet firmness underlay her words.

Shue sighed.

"I know you have no aspirations, you've always preferred simplicity, but now that I've mentioned it to you, I hope that you will take my words into consideration. You have nothing to fear when I am governor, but I am not getting any younger. If anything happens…"

"No," Hong said firmly. "Master, please don't speak about it. You are in the prime of your life, and you still have many, many years ahead."

Normally a servant would not speak like this in front of her master, but Shue was not like most masters. He had been friends with Hong's father, and even offered to adopt her when Hong's father fell in favour at court. But according to the law, Hong was and should remain low class. She was truly fortunate that Shue had taken her under his wing, for servants were mere commodities and could be easily bartered and sold.

Were Hong a normal servant, she would have acquiesced. She did not even desire the prestigious status of a first wife, she was willing to become Fang's concubine, bear him children, and indulge herself in music and poetry. But since she spent much of her time taking out criminals, settling down was unthinkable. She did not want to endanger the Shue family or her future children.

Shue picked up his brush with another sigh. He had been considering asking Hong to renounce her vigilante identity, but she had made it clear that she did not want to find a partner. Poor Fang. He had known his third son was attracted to Hong, but as far as he could see, the maid did not reciprocate.

"Just think about it, Hong. I honestly believe it's the best for you."

Hong immediately felt remorse. It was not as if Shue was forcing her to yield to some undesirable man thrice her age.

"I apologise, master." She bowed her head. "I will heed your words and let you know when I am ready to be wed." But it definitely wouldn't be soon, and it wouldn't happen while she was still in Shue's residence.

"Good." Shue looked relieved. "Fang has told me that Master Liu is going to teach you a new song for the upcoming banquet. How about you practise your music with him? I'll be occupied with state affairs, so he can serve in my place when you need to have someone listen in advance—apart from Liu, of course. Fang is more versed in music than I am."

Hong could not help but smile a little at Shue's attempt to create opportunities for his son. Well, that request she could meet.

"Yes, master."

Hong was thankful that no big mission came up, which meant that she spent a lot of time at Old Man Liu's doing exactly what everyone expected her to be doing: practising the song for Shue's birthday. Liu had picked a flute song for her, a light and cheery melody that would go well with Shue's birthday banquet. While Hong was more used to practising sad, mournful tunes that brought tears to many a listener, she made the effort to master the song.

She did not neglect her training, however. Old Man Liu continued to drill her mercilessly; he increased the number of candles she had to extinguish twofold and threefold, he made her go running up and down the hill in the back of the compound. In the unlikely case that someone was to drop by again, Liu could just say that Hong was improving her stamina for her music performance.

"That's why I picked the flute," he said gruffly. "You need to possess strength in your abdomen to perform well."

Hong didn't answer. She was still worn out from making twenty trips up and down the hill.

"However, you're seriously limited by your body," Liu said. "No matter how much training you do, you won't last as long as a well-trained fighter, and you'll never beat the strength of a man. A weak scholar, no problem. But a man who's used to hard labour can easily beat you in an arm wrestle, not to mention one who has undergone serious martial arts training."

Hong looked down. "No hope?"

"Nope. Ask Meng-Ting, he's the physician, he knows the human anatomy. Unless..." Liu snapped his fingers. "Unless we can get hold of the Lost

Manual, I'd say you have zero chance outperforming a man in strength and stamina."

"The Lost Manual?" Hong frowned.

"Just a nickname, since it's obviously not been in existence for some time," Liu said. "What I know of is this: the Manual instructs on the training of the Water Fist. It is a secret scroll that employs the wisdom of our ancients. When one masters the training, one will master the power of water."

Liu picked up his teacup from his armrest. He tipped the cup over, allowing a few drops to spill on the stone pavement of the court yard.

"You see that water, which seems so soft and malleable, is actually strong enough to create a crack in stone, provided it drips long enough? That is the power the Manual claims. A person from the Hard School of Training, like the Shaolin Monks, can break a slab of stone with a single tough blow. The stone will fall apart in two pieces from the impact. But one who has mastered the Water Fist can break the stone through a different kind of strength. The sound of the palm hitting the stone is not loud, but the stone will gradually crumble into several smaller pieces."

Hong refilled the teacup and pressed it into Liu's hand. "So no one knows where the Lost Manual is now?"

"No idea," Liu croaked. "Last fighter who knew the Water Fist had died—a Taoist nun, I think. No children, of course, and if she had any disciples, they certainly are keeping a low profile."

Hong thought for a moment. For the year that she had worked as a vigilante, she had not met any fighter who possessed the unique skill Liu mentioned. The possibility of cracking—no, crumbling—a stone by force sounded wildly far-fetched, yet she knew her *sifu* would never lie to her.

Liu set his cup down with a thud on the stone floor. "Forget about it," he commanded. "Your martial skills are decent enough, and if you use your head and weapons wisely, there are few who can be a worthy opponent. I am only concerned that if a time comes when you have to singlehandedly defeat an army, or several first-class fighters, your stamina would be a weakness. You'd do well to end a fight as soon as possible."

Hong nodded but did not speak. Even though Liu was blind, she knew that he was able to hear her nodding by sensing the slight change in the air around him.

"Well, get out your lute," Liu said abruptly. "Who knows when your lover boy might pay another visit?"

"Young Master Fang is not my lover, *sifu*."

Liu grunted. "I may be old, but I can tell that no young man of privilege is going to trudge all the way from the city here on foot."

Hong was silent. A light breeze ruffled her hair.

"So what are you going to do about him?"

She looked down on the ground. "Nothing."

Liu puckered his brows. "Hmph. I knew I taught you sense. Most young men are fools—I was a fool myself—but for a young man of his rank and privilege, he seems decent enough. However, what'll he say if he knows what you've been doing? You can conceal your identity for now, but you can't hide it forever. And even if he accepts you for who you are, it'll be dangerous for him. He'll worry for your safety, and you'll worry about not surviving to grow old with him. And if you have children, that'll be the end. You can never be a vigilante."

Hong knew these things well enough; she had thought about them a long time ago. "I know."

"Better make it soon."

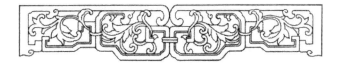

7

Back at Shue's residence, Hong was again at her daily chores. Excitement was brewing as the entire compound prepared for Shue's banquet. There was the feast, of course, and festive activities like shooting contests, drinking games, and music performances.

After finishing breakfast, which consisted of simple white rice, a boiled egg and some pickles, she headed towards the main compound for her usual morning ritual of cleaning.

On her way, she heard the sound of swords clashing near the lotus pond. An audience consisting of both chambermaids and manservants were gathered around two young men fighting.

When Hong neared the crowd, she saw that it was Fang and his second elder brother, Ping.

"How come they are having a duel?" Hong asked Golden Lotus, who was chewing on her handkerchief.

"Master Fang is going to perform a sword dance during the banquet, and Master Ping, who was passing by, challenged him." Golden Lotus looked on the verge of tearing her handkerchief in half. "Oh, Hong, who do you think will win?"

Hong looked accordingly. While she was more familiar with a dagger than the long sword, the acuity she had acquired from years of training enabled her to make judgement immediately.

Ping was about five years older than Fang, though slightly shorter and had a more muscular build. His movements were calculated and precise; Fang had to rely on his reflexes to parry the blows in the last second. On the other hand, Fang moved faster with a greater burst of energy, his sword thrusts making whipping sounds in the wind. Yet from the sheen of sweat on his neck and his soaked collar, it appeared that he was expending a lot more energy in the duel. He would certainly lose, but Hong privately thought that given his age and experience, it was a remarkable thing that he had managed to hold his own for so long.

Since she already knew the outcome and that she ought not neglect her duties, Hong turned to leave. She had only gone several paces when there was another loud clang of swords meeting, and someone cried out.

Without her looking back, her acute hearing detected something small hurtling in her direction with lightning speed. She knew not what the flying object was, but she sensed it was going to hit the back of her head.

She couldn't risk getting hit; who knew when Old Man Liu would have a new mission? Yet she couldn't reach out and snatch the object either, it would give away her martial abilities. No normal person, even with a stroke of luck, could catch a whizzing object without turning around.

In a split second, Hong made a show of tripping forward. Something hit her chignon—she usually fashioned her hair in a simple chignon on top of her head, as was the usual hairstyle for girls.

"Hong!" Fang and Golden Lotus cried out.

Slowly, Hong extricated the flying object from her hair. It was a small jagged piece of steel broken off from the sword. The edges and tip were sharp; she knew Fang and his brothers regularly had their swords sharpened and polished.

Fang rushed over to her, looking concerned. "Hong, are you all right?"

She nodded and hid her face in her hands, her shoulders trembling. It would look strange if she displayed no fear. Golden Lotus put an arm around her shoulders.

"I should have been more careful," Fang said angrily. "If that sword point had hit your head, it would have done great damage."

Hong shook her head. "It's all right," she said softly. "Sometimes accidents happen."

"It's extremely fortunate that you tripped," Ping said, looking at her. "Well, Fang, I think you've proved yourself well accomplished in your sword training. However, remember it's not enough just to be strong and fast—you have to use your brain as well. My strength may not measure up to yours, but since I controlled the angle where I hit, I was able to break your sword."

Something in his tone made Hong wary. Had he been deliberately aiming at her when he broke the sword?

"I see. Thanks for your input, brother, I'll be sure to watch out next time. Do we have wooden swords? I think we need to keep our practising to safer weapons for now on."

"That wouldn't work," Ping replied. "The weight and feel of the wooden sword is completely different. It might have sufficed when we were children and starting to learn the craft, but if you are serious about your training, use the real thing. Your opponents won't be using wooden toys in a real war."

Fang flushed. There was a slight note of condescension in Ping's tone, as though Fang were still a child. "But Hong isn't a warrior." Fang glanced at the slender maidservant who barely reached over his shoulders. "And neither are our other servants. It would be plain wrong to sacrifice them because of an accident."

Hong had a sudden rush of affection for her young master/childhood friend; very few noble young men were as considerate as him. Though at the same time, she was inclined to laugh when he said she wasn't a warrior. He fought well, definitely, but she doubted he could evade a torrent of darts.

"We'll discuss this matter later," Ping said, with another glance at Hong. "Run along, Hong, Father will be needing you in his study. Golden Lotus, go and fetch us some chilled wine. There's nothing like a cup of sweet wine from Family Luo's cellar on a warm day like this."

Hong slipped away quietly, her heart pounding. She had witnessed many sword duels between the brothers, but rarely did the swords break. She wondered if Ping had done it on purpose. He was more observant and harder to fool. Perhaps, after

Shue's banquet, she had better hurry up and find an excuse to leave the governor's residence.

The banquet for Shue's fiftieth birthday was held with great splendour. As he was the military governor of the district, many generals and army officers were invited. The magistrate was also present, with his wife and two concubines. Several prominent mandarins, scholars, and even a couple of merchants attended.

Food and drink were served in silver platters, though portions were not as large as expected. Shue had been trying to reduce the extravagance of expenses, especially after the An Lushan rebellion, which had seriously damaged the Tang Empire. It was not hard to see where Fang got his altruistic behaviour.

After a round of drinking and bantering, Shue rose.

"My friends, I thank you all for honouring me with your presence today." He smiled and made eye contact with the guests all around. "Now that you have eaten and drunk your fill, it is time for entertainment. I propose that we start with some music. My personal assistant, Hong Sien, is an accomplished flute player, who had the privilege of being schooled by the great Master Liu himself. Master Liu, as you no doubt know, came from the Pear Garden troupe that served the emperor. We may not be in the imperial court, but we shall also have the chance to partake in a music performance fit for the emperor."

Amid tumultuous applause, Hong walked to the centre of the room, where a stool of black ebony was placed, draped with a piece of crimson silk. She was wearing a rose-pink brocaded dress with a pale yellow scarf wound over her sleeves and falling to the floor. A single pink peony was pinned in her hair; silver hoop earrings glittered on her ear lobes. Her eyebrows were plucked and painted, her face snowy white from rice powder. Her flute—a long slender instrument of high-quality jade—was attached to the sash tied around her waist.

There were murmurs of approval from the audience. Fang sat with a frown on his face. He thought Hong looked nice, but the white rice paint made her look too artificial, like some doll. Moreover, he did not like the way some of the generals ogled her, despite Hong being fully dressed. Many of the women present wore low-necked robes that showed plenty of skin—why couldn't they keep their eyes fixed on those women instead?

Hong dipped in a curtsy and turned around, her expression demure and respectful. Raising her hands, which were doused in scented water, she began to play.

The melody was light-hearted and playful, quite apt for the song's name, *A Walk in Springtime*. Soon people began to tap on the table or clap their hands, keeping to the rhythm of the music. Hong's fingers moved expertly on the flute, the rhythm getting quicker and quicker. Finally the tune reached its pinnacle, finishing on the highest note on the flute. Then the song ended.

Silence ensued. A few people were still transfixed, as though they could not believe that the song had ended. Then applause broke out; people were shouting and cheering and raising their goblets to Hong.

"Who is that girl?" a general was whispering. "She isn't as beautiful as my wife, but that music is splendid! D'you think Shue will yield her if I ask him?"

"Better not," his companion replied. "I've heard that this girl has enjoyed special favour in the Shue residence—Shue will be taking her as his concubine any time. I suppose he wants to wait until she's old enough."

"Too bad." The general sat back with a sigh. "Old Shue wasn't lying when he said she was schooled by Master Liu."

"You greedy lout!" another officer said. "You already have a beautiful wife, and your concubine is a skilled dancer. Now you want another? Never satisfied, huh?"

"A man is like a teapot, Sergeant Kong," the general said. "A teapot needs several teacups to be a complete set. Likewise, my wife has already fulfilled her role of being ornamental, my concubine satisfies my desire for a good performance, so a girl like this can enhance the musical quality of life... ow!"

Hot mulled wine spilt on his table, wetting his sleeves.

"Very sorry, General Su," Fang said, grabbing a cloth and dabbing at his sleeve. "This wine jar's handle is too flimsy, it just slipped before I could control it. Can I fetch you a new robe?"

"Oh, don't worry about it," General Su said, wringing his own sleeves with a hasty, rough motion. "It'll dry in a minute. What a pity—that wine was excellent quality. Just mind you watch your grip next time... I suppose you don't drink that much? Don't have much experience handling wine containers, hey?"

Fang resented Su's patronising tone, but he knew better than to retort in an inflamed manner.

"Not much, General," he said, trying to sound nonchalant. "Now I've learnt a lesson."

General Su guffawed and reached for another wine jar. "Here, drink up! We'll make a man outta ya, Fang!"

Hong performed a second song, due to great demand from the guests, but then she declined a third request, excusing herself to rest and take some refreshments. She settled on a stool near Shue and poured herself some water.

Then came a game of pot-pitching, in which a copper pot with a narrow opening was placed in the centre of the room. Each guest was given a handful of arrows, and they were invited to toss their arrows into the pot. Whoever had the most arrows would be awarded a prize.

Hong sat quietly and sipped her water. Arrows flew fast and thick, raining on the pot. Some of the guests were clearly skilled, while others failed even to hit the pot itself. Not only the male guests were allowed to throw; some of the wives and concubines were also given the chance, though only Lynn did well. Everyone applauded and expressed that one couldn't expect less from a military governor's daughter.

"Hong, would you like to try?" Shue asked. "Just for fun."

Hong smiled but declined. With her ability to extinguish candles, it would be too easy to outperform everyone. Still, she could not help observing keenly how the guests took aim—the angle they chose, the positioning of the arrows, the movements of their arms.

As it turned out, Chiao-Ming, a champion archer and experienced fighter, took the prize. Chiao-Ming was a three-time champion in the annual archery contests, and he was famous for having subdued two drunken men with knives when he himself was unarmed.

Then it was time for Fang's sword dance. Shue's three sons took turns to perform a sword dance on his birthday, and this year happened to be Fang's turn. The sword dance consisted of a choreographed routine performed to music. Given the military nature of the dance, the music was produced by drums.

Nervous yet determined, Fang walked to the centre of the room. Slowly, he drew out his sword and unsheathed it. The polished steel gleamed and flashed in the sunlight.

Seven soldiers with seven military drums lined up on one side. Once Fang unsheathed his sword, the soldiers began to drum.

Swish went the sword, as Fang did a variety of kicks and jumps and slices. His movements were mostly powerful and fluid; while some of the sword moves were not performed to perfection, one could predict that the young man had potential.

Hong also watched with an appreciative eye. She was more used to the dagger than sword, but she could tell a good swordsman when she saw one. Fang *was* good, though it was obvious that he lacked experience. The practice duels with his brother were not enough; he needed real fights in order to be accustomed to reacting immediately. The moves of the sword dance were carefully choreographed, but in fights, one could not just perform the moves one by one.

Bong, bong, went the drums. Hong matched the beat of the drums to Fang's movements, noting how well the beats matched to his moves, but after a while, she sensed that something was wrong. Although most of the drumming was performed in a uniform manner, one of the drums sounded distorted.

She looked at the soldiers drumming; one of them kept his face down with his brows knitted, as opposed to the rest of them, who were grinning and keeping up to Fang's performance. All the other guests were concentrated on Fang.

Hong closed her eyes temporarily. Years of training with Old Man Liu had not only made her sensitive to noises of weapons in the dark, but also to music itself. Her facade was not merely a mask of her martial skills; she was still an accomplished musical performer.

Yes, there was definitely an uneven beat in the drumming. Very slight, hardly perceptible, but it was there.

Hong opened her eyes. The song had come to an end.

"Master?" she whispered to Shue Song. "I believe one of the soldiers drumming has a problem. He does not dare to speak of it, but his mood is expressed through his drumming."

A normal master might have ridiculed her comment. Shue, however, had some musical background himself, and he always appreciated Hong's expertise, so he merely asked, "Which one is it?"

"The second soldier to the left—the one with a mole on the corner of his mouth."

Shue beckoned to another servant, who swiftly went to the drummers. The soldier who Hong had noticed came forward and fell to his knees.

"Beg pardon, Master Shue! I did not mean to be inattentive to my job, especially on such an important occasion as today."

Fang, who had sheathed his sword and was wiping his neck with a handkerchief, noticed the man kneeling in front of his father. It was Chow, his face pale and his lip trembling.

"No need to panic, Chow," Shue said. "My maid has detected that you seem not to be yourself today. I merely wish to enquire if things are all right with you."

Chow flushed and looked down. Shue's benevolent tone put him at ease.

"My... my wife just passed away yesterday."

Fang's eyes widened. Opal was... *dead*? It couldn't be.

"Then you should not be here," Shue said, and waved his hand. "This is no small matter. Go home this instant and take care of the burial and funeral."

Chow bowed. There was a relieved expression on his face as he took his leave.

"Excellent hearing, Hong," Shue said in a low voice. Then he stood up and said, "Now let us commence with the next performance!"

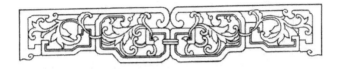

8

Fang weaved through the streets of the city, heading for Chow's residence. He wondered how he hadn't noticed Chow's change of mood that day; perhaps he had been too occupied with his preparations for his sword dance performance. Thanks to Hong, they had spared Chow from trying to appear cheerful on a day he should be mourning.

A warm glow rose in his heart when he thought of Hong and her flute performance during the festivities. She had looked lovely in the pink dress; it suited her far better than the dull, dark blue robe she wore every day. Briefly he wondered about buying a new dress for her—but then, would she accept? He knew she never expressed a desire for pretty dresses and jewellery—but still, he would like to get nice things for her.

Then his thoughts returned to his friend. Why had Opal died so suddenly? Had that devil of a magistrate's son molested her again? Maybe she had committed suicide because she couldn't remain faithful to her husband. Something in the back of his mind felt that it wasn't that simple, though. While Opal wasn't forceful by nature, it didn't seem to him that she lacked courage. She had the nerve to go to the northwest district where brothels and winehouses were plenty—a district normally considered unfit for a married woman to visit.

It was unfortunate that she had died so young. She couldn't have been more than twenty. Moreover, he was worried about Chow. Though Chow was only of an ordinary rank, he was only a few years older than Fang. They had often hunted and duelled together. When Chow had got married, Fang had been invited as a special guest. Who would have known that the marriage just a year ago would have ended in such a brutal way?

He reached Chow's house. It was located on a pretty street lined with drooping willow trees. Everything was peaceful, save for a few children playing with a shuttlecock outside, kicking it back and forth between them. The neighbourhood seemed safe and tranquil, an agreeable place for a young couple.

The door was open. Still, Fang rapped twice before entering.

Inside was a main room with a dining table and low benches. A door to the right opened to the bedroom, while the other on the left led to the kitchen. In the main room, a small table stood on one side of the wall. Two candles, white for mourning, burned on the table.

Chow was slumped against the dining table, barely looking up when Fang entered.

"It's me."

Chow raised his head. His eyes were red and puffy, he had dark circles under his eyes, and from the wrinkled state of his clothes, it seemed he hadn't changed at all since yesterday.

"Good heavens, man," Fang exclaimed, genuinely alarmed. He looked around for some water, and found a brass tea kettle lying overturned in a corner. Quickly, he picked up the kettle and went to the back yard. He had been to Chow's place before and knew there was a well in the yard. Using the bucket in the well, he filled the kettle with water and returned.

"Here." Fang set a cup of fresh water before Chow. "You need to freshen up. Have you made the necessary preparations for the funeral?"

Slowly, Chow nodded. "The neighbours helped," he croaked.

"Good." Fang wished there was something he could do. "I'm really sorry, Chow. Father said that you're to take the next week off. Just let us know when you're... you're ready to return."

Chow said nothing; he simply stared ahead. Fang decided to simply pay his respects to the deceased and leave. He took up the incense lying on the small table, lit them using the white candles, and prayed that Opal would rest in peace.

"I don't understand," Chow suddenly said.

"Huh?"

"Do you know how my wife died?" Chow's eyes were full of anguish. "She was killed, Fang! When I came home the day before, she was sitting on the floor right there"—he pointed at the wall—"with a knife run clean through her chest. It was awful." He laid his head back on the table, his shoulders shaking.

A chill ran down Fang's spine. He wondered if he should mention Ho Jiang-Min, but decided against it for now.

"Are you sure it was murder?" he managed to say. "Was it not possible that she took her own life instead?"

"Why would she want to take her life? She didn't have any cause for it. Besides, I have never seen the knife on her body. It wasn't a kitchen knife; it was a dagger. The kind that assassins use, I believe." Chow looked towards the small table that held his wife's things. "I've questioned the neighbours," he said. "but they haven't been able to shed any light. We just moved to this part of town two months ago when I saved enough—I don't believe Opal made any enemies around here. Maybe a quarrel sometimes with the neighbours, but nothing serious enough to warrant murder."

"What about her past acquaintances?"

"I can't say I know much about them," Chow said, running a hand through his hair. "We met through a matchmaker; all I know is that before our marriage, she worked as a maidservant for the magistrate's daughter."

Fang put a hand under his chin. "Has she been keeping in contact with anyone from her former workplace?"

"None that I know of. She didn't like to talk about her past, and I didn't want to pressure her. When we got married, I had the feeling that she wanted to put her life at the magistrate's behind her and start anew."

Just then, they heard a couple voices at the door.

"Is this the place of Mrs. Chow? Wait a bit... she's dead, you say? Impossible!"

In burst a large, bulky middle-aged woman. She was gaudily dressed in a red silk brocaded robe, with a large fake red peony stuck in her hair. The three children Fang had seen playing in the streets hovered in the doorway, looking on curiously.

Fang stood up, unsure of what to say. He had never seen her before.

"May I help you?"

"Is it true that Mrs. Chow is dead?" the woman demanded.

Fang pointed at the small table. The white candles should be proof enough, not to mention the miserable husband.

The woman let out a sound of frustration, and stomped on the ground with one foot. "Damn it!"

By now, Chow had regained his composure. "Who are you? Do you know my wife? What business have you with her?"

"So you're her husband, eh?" The woman gave Chow an appraising look. "Well, you seem a decent sort. I am Madam Jin; my husband owns the huge gambling house on the Second Main Street, and I the Heavenly Pleasure Quarters, the biggest brothel in town. I don't suppose she told you that she owes me a good deal of money?"

"No!" Chow snapped. "She wasn't in debt! I provided everything she needed."

"Obviously she hasn't told you," Madam Jin said with contempt. Reaching in her robes, she brought out several pieces of paper, folded carefully. Keeping enough distance from Fang and Chow, she unfolded one paper and displayed it.

"See here? Your wife's signature," she announced, pointing to the right-hand corner. "She played a game of dice and lost in our gambling house four months ago—three thousand silver taels! So far she has only paid up two-thirds of the amount."

"My wife never went gambling!" Chow shouted, pounding his fist on the table. "What a ridiculous claim! You must have forged her signature!"

Madam Jin took a step backwards, but her expression remained defiant.

"Ask anyone at the gambling house," she said, tossing her head. "They'll tell you that on May fourth, the day before the Dragon Boat Festival, your wife came to our house. Originally I thought of refusing her, she didn't look like she could pay up, but she's pretty enough to fetch some gold in the brothel. Don't look at me like that, you fool! Plenty of husbands and fathers do the same, and I've seen many a wife and daughter come beg me for a good word at Heavenly Pleasures so they can pay off their debts."

Fang had to keep a tight hold on Chow to prevent him from leaping at Madam Jin.

"Did she…?" he said in a coarse whisper. "Did my wife… did she end up…?"

Madam Jin laughed shrilly. "Just like a man! Worried that her working at a brothel would stain your reputation, more than worrying how *she'd* feel to work there. No wonder she didn't come to you for aid. But you're in luck—your wife happened to have some rare scrolls of poetry that could be sold for a large amount of money. Never thought that an uncultured little maid like her would be in possession of such art! I suppose that her former employment at the magistrate yielded them."

"My wife isn't the literary type," Chow said, though it seemed more like talking to himself. "I've never seen the books you've mentioned."

Madam Jin snorted. "Right. And you never knew she was in debt either." She looked hard at him. "So. A thousand taels of silver left. Care to tell me how you gonna pay up?"

A thousand taels was no small sum. Chow himself only made about a hundred taels every month, and most of his savings were spent paying for the new house he bought when he got married.

"Two hundred and thirty taels," he said. "That's all I have now."

Madam Jin clucked her tongue. "You sure you cannot raise more? Nothing valuable you can pawn? Our interest rates are quite high, I'm warning you."

"Here." Fang removed the jade belt hook that Shu-Mo advised him about, and handed it to her. "This is made of the finest jade imported from Yu-Tien. This will fetch three hundred taels at least. I'll come by the gambling house to pay the rest, once I assemble it."

"Fang!" Chow tried to stop him, but Madam Jin had already snatched the jade pendent.

"You can pay me back later, you've already had enough to deal with," Fang hissed.

Madam Jin had finished her lightning-fast inspection of the jade. She must have had plenty of experience with valuables anyway. "This looks genuine," she admitted. "But how am I going to have proof that you will pay the rest?"

"I'll sign a deed," Fang said readily. "If I can't assemble the amount within three days, you're welcome to raise the debt. I'm the governor's son, it'll be easy to find me."

Madam Jin raised her eyebrows. "The governor's son! I should have known."

But she still made him draw up a deed and sign it with his signature and thumb mark. Fang made her rip up Opal's debt as well, lest she used it to bother Chow in the future.

When Fang finished the deed, Madam Jin snatched it and put it in her bosom pocket.

"Make sure you pay up in three days," she warned Fang. "You might be the governor's son, but we've been in the gambling business for twenty years, we know how to make people pay. If you want, I can arrange a discreet time and place where we can meet. That's how Opal managed to keep her debt from her husband. Speaking of the poor girl, was it a disease that carried her off? Or was she run down by a carriage?"

Chow ignored her. Fang, however, saw an opportunity to learn more about Opal's death. He whispered in Chow's ear, and finally the latter nodded.

"She was murdered," he said, spitting out the word 'murder' as though it were a disease itself. "Have you any clue who might have done it?"

Madam Jin widened her small beady eyes. "How tragic! Well, I wish I knew, but I've only known your wife since she came to our gambling house. She was very secretive, that one. Why don't you enquire at the magistrate's place? They'll be much more knowledgeable about her past. And don't look at me like that! Would I kill her when she hasn't even paid up the full amount?" She took her leave, stomping on her way out.

There was a long silence after they heard her slam the door. Fang and Chow looked at each other.

"I'll pay you back," Chow said, staring at the wall.

"I'll make sure you will," Fang said, clapping a hand on his back. "But first I think we'd better ascertain who killed your wife, may her soul rest in peace. So you really have no clue who might have done it?"

Chow clenched his fists. "I'd have gone out and sought the murderer if I knew who it was."

"Leave it to me," Fang said. "You take care of the funeral and other stuff. I'll go and ask around, and I'll let you know what I've found. We won't let her death be shrouded in mystery."

9

Back in his room, Fang paced up and down. He debated whether to visit the Guo residence and ask for Ho Wen-Jun, the magistrate's daughter. The first time he'd seen Opal was when he had been a guest at the magistrate's compound. She had still been a servant there then. But since Wen-Jun was recently married, it did not seem decent to ask to see her, especially considering his single status.

Finally, he decided that he would go to the magistrate's compound instead. He knew a couple of maidservants, or rather, he was sure that they would recognise him—there was a girl called Little Jade who had presented him a small silken pouch with her own embroidery, filled with dried flowers and herbs. Surely they would have some information about Opal.

The door flung open. Shu-Mo stumbled inside, his face flushed and his eyes bright and excited.

"Young Master—I need your opinion this time." Shu-Mo straightened the lower folds of his neat white robe. "Do you think this looks good on me? Or should I put on my sky-blue robe instead?"

Fang laughed. How similar Shu-Mo was to him, just a couple of weeks earlier.

"I don't think the colour makes much of a difference," he said. "But I do think that you ought to put all your hair up in a top knot and bind it tightly with a cloth cap—it'll make you look better groomed. Besides, you don't want messy hair flying in your face if a wind comes up."

"No problem," Shu-Mo said. "I'm glad I just bought a new cap."

"So who's the lady?" Fang said. "Someone you met at Father's banquet?"

Shu-Mo went a bright shade of red. "It's one of the maids accompanying the magistrate's wife. She must be recently employed. I haven't seen her when we visited before."

"Well, now that's a coincidence!" Fang clapped his shoulder. "I was just planning to go to the magistrate's today." His expression turned sober. "I need to find out more regarding Opal, Chow's wife."

Shu-Mo's mouth fell open. "Why?"

Briefly, Fang explained what he had seen and heard at Chow's house the day before. As he spoke, Shu-Mo's eyes grew bigger and bigger.

"Opal was killed by someone unknown? How terrible!" And his shoulders shook. "I can't believe it. She had always seemed—friendly. I liked her."

Fang set his jaw. "That is why I am going to find out who killed her. Chow is already a wreck. I might as well find something useful to do."

"I'll come with you," Shu-Mo immediately said. "And I'll have a perfect excuse to visit!"

Master and servant headed towards the stables together. The head of the stables was a half-Turk with bronze skin, muscular stature, and pronounced features. The nomadic Turks were known for their ability to handle horses; many of them, besides dealing in animal trading with the Chinese people, were also employed to take care of grooming and training horses.

"Saddle my mount, and also a horse for Shu-Mo," Fang instructed. "We'll be going to the magistrate's compound today."

The Turk bowed. "Right away, Young Master."

"Going to the magistrate's?"

Shue Gwang, Fang's eldest brother, leaned against the wooden railing at a corner. He was of medium height and build, with a laid-back attitude and a ready smile. By his feet lay a handsome red leather quiver, full of arrows, and a large polished bow of the finest quality.

"I thought you'd be at Chow's today, helping out with the funeral stuff. Otherwise I'd ask if you'd join me on a wild hunt today."

"Chow has already enlisted help from the neighbours," Fang said. He would have told Gwang about Opal's murder, but he didn't feel like going through the explanation again. He could fill in the details after he got enough information from the magistrate's maidservants.

"Kind of unlucky that the tragedy happened around Father's banquet," Gwang said, with a shrug of his shoulders. "But I say, it's kind of unbelievable that Hong 'managed to *hear* his grief through his drumming. We know that she's pretty accomplished in music, being trained by Old Man Liu and all, but

71

detecting hidden emotion from the sound and beat of drums? Perhaps I should pay her more attention— she keeps such a low profile that I never noticed her before."

"Master Gwang!" Shu-Mo was quick to stand up for his master. "About Hong..." He made a gesture at Fang and winked.

Gwang got the message. "Ah, forget what I said," he grinned. "Well, I had better be off. I think I'll stop at Chow's to pay my respects. Maybe pass along some game to him, if the hunt goes well. Now, where does he live?"

Riding to the magistrate's house actually cost more time than Fang had expected. There were street performers juggling knives on one road, attracting a huge crowd. The law decreed that no rider could race into a crowd of more than five people, so he couldn't ride as fast as he liked.

When they did reach their destination, Fang and Shu-Mo did a double take. The double gates of red lacquer were so huge that ten people could enter at the same time, the high wall that ran around the compound was so long that one had to squint to see where it ended, and the roofs of the buildings were heavily decorated with green-glazed dragons and clouds and tree tops.

"When was the last time we were here?" Shu-Mo said, craning his neck. "Master, look at that pair of dragons carved on the rooftop! Are those real pearls for their eyes?"

"Hmm. Must be the result of his being the emperor's father-in-law," Fang muttered. The magistrate had certainly done well in marrying off his daughters. The eldest, who was rumoured to be a remarkable beauty, had been bundled off and sent to the emperor's harem when she was twelve. Recently, at the age of twenty, she had been promoted to the high rank of Grand Concubine, a title second only to the queen. The second daughter, Wen-Jun, was also beautiful. However, her weak constitution had led her to remain at home. Still, she had ended up marrying Guo Yen-Bin, the son of the most successful businessman in the city. No wonder Magistrate Ho's place now looked like a palatial mansion.

Fang dismounted with fluidity and grace. He straightened the front of his robe and strode up to the double doors. Lifting the heavy brass ring on the door, he knocked twice.

The door creaked open. Two burly guards dressed in grey uniforms looked out.

"Good morning. My name is Shue Fang," Fang said. "Is the magistrate home?"

"He has gone to the polo field today," the guard replied. "You have to come back in the evening. The games tend to take all day."

"That is not a problem. As a matter of fact, I'd like to speak with some of the maidservants."

The guard regarded him with a wary expression. "Young man, if you are seeking pleasure, the brothels are located on the other side of town."

"You misunderstand my intentions," Fang said, trying not to show irritation. "I merely wish to derive information of one of your former maids who served Miss Ho—I mean, Mrs. Guo now."

"Idiot!" The other guard elbowed the first one. "It's the governor's son, didn't you hear his name? Do you think he'd lack maidservants in his own home?"

Making a bow to Fang, the second guard said, "Which maid would you like to speak to, Mr. Shue?"

"Little Jade." She was one of Mrs. Guo's two closest maids. The other one being Opal, of course.

"She's no longer here. Gone with the mistress when she married Merchant Guo's son."

"Oh." Fang scratched his head. He remembered a few faces, but couldn't remember their names. The last time he visited here was what—six months ago? Or more?

"Can we see... Miss Pearl?" Shu-Mo suddenly said. A pink hue graced his cheeks; Fang instantly guessed that this must be the girl with whom Shu-Mo had fallen in love.

"If it isn't too much trouble," Fang added. He didn't think seeing Pearl would be much use, since she was new, but he wanted to give Shu-Mo a chance. Plus, he was curious to see the girl who had captivated his servant's heart.

A while later, with the help of another male servant, they arrived at the garden. It was densely planted with bamboos and willow trees, huge rocks erected to look like the mountains in watercolour paintings, so that it looked almost like a maze. A rounded archway stood at the end of the garden. When Fang had accompanied Lynn, his younger sister, who was friends with the magistrate's daughter, he had had to stop outside the archway, which presumably led to the women's quarters. While it wasn't forbidden for women folk to interact with men, the magistrate was known to be assiduous in upholding his younger daughter's reputation, especially when she was stunningly beautiful. It would be a great insult if the Grand Concubine's younger sister was known to be loose with men.

"Please wait here. I will summon Pearl," the male servant said. He went to the archway and called, "A guest from the governor's has come. Is Pearl in there? Tell her to come out."

Fang sat down in a pavilion near the archway. Shu-Mo leaned against one of the wooden pillars of the pavilion. Back at home, he would have sat down with Fang, but here at the magistrate's, he had to act like any other servant.

"Master Shue Fang?" An excited female voice echoed in the garden. "Oh! It really is you!"

A pretty young girl around sixteen came running down to the pavilion. She wore a light yellow robe and had red ribbons in her shiny black hair. Another girl dressed in a pink skirt and white top followed her rather hesitantly.

"Little Jade?" Fang rose to meet her, surprised at her appearance. "I thought you had moved to Merchant Guo's with your mistress."

"Oh, I just dropped by to get some things. I'll be heading back soon. Oh, it has been *such* a while, Master Shue! I'm so glad to see you." Little Jade looked as though she wanted to grasp his arm, but since he offered no encouragement, she had to settle for gazing at him adoringly.

"Er... I suppose," Fang said lamely. In the corner of his eye, he glimpsed Shu-Mo approaching the other girl slowly, as though he were afraid she'd turn on her heel and run off if he were too eager. Pearl was also pretty, though a bit taller than Shu-Mo, and probably older as well, but there was a gentleness in her eyes that reminded him slightly of Hong. Like master, like servant, he thought wryly.

"Master Shue?" Little Jade waved a delicate silk handkerchief in front of his face. The Guos certainly were affluent enough if they could provide their servants with silken goods. "Did you come here on an errand for the governor?"

Fang cleared his throat. "Little Jade, do you know that Opal... what happened to her?"

"Opal?" Little Jade tilted her head, a suspicious look in her eyes. "Why are you asking me? Wasn't she married to one of the soldiers at Governor Shue's?"

Fang briefly explained about the unfortunate maid's death. Since Opal's death was pretty recent and Chow hadn't held her funeral yet, it was reasonable that Little Jade hadn't heard the news.

Immediately, Little Jade's suspicion turned into pity.

"Oh! I cannot believe it... she seemed so capable of taking care of herself. Poor Opal! She didn't leave a child behind, did she?"

"No. In fact," Fang lowered his voice to a whisper, "we believe that her death was unnatural."

Little Jade's hand flew to her mouth. "You mean she was killed?" Fortunately, she also kept her voice low.

Fang looked around. Shu-Mo and Pearl had disappeared somewhere; it was quite easy to do so when there were so many rocks and bushes in the garden.

"Yes. There was a knife on her body."

"Oh!" Little Jade looked horrified. "So this is why you came here?"

"I had thought of going to Mrs. Guo, but since she is married," Fang shrugged, "I figured I had better come here first."

"Well…" Little Jade twisted her fingers. "To tell you the truth, I really have no clue who might want Opal dead."

"She had no enemies?"

"Not really; she wasn't well liked, but I don't think anyone would have wanted to kill her. When I arrived, I heard some maids saying they disliked her, because she slept with Master Jiang-Min in exchange for money."

Fang frowned. So that explained why Jiang-Min was molesting Opal in the alley. Fang might not be the most worldly person, but he knew that a woman was never regarded with respect if she used her body for financial gain.

"Oh, and there was Mr. Yao," Little Jade added.

"Mr. Yao?"

"Yao Chian—that's his full name—he also worked for us before. He was a bodyguard. A big, strong man, though it was a pity he didn't turn out well."

"What do you mean?"

"Well, he used to be a decent fellow until he took up drinking. He was already pretty strong—I once saw him lift up a sick cow with his bare hands and deposit it on a cart. Opal said that he was like a different person when he was drunk. He'd get mad easily and took his frustration out with his fists. Once he beat up a scholar so badly, we had to call several men to restrain him. I think it's because of his violence the magistrate had to dismiss him, even if he was the best fighter among all the bodyguards."

"I see," Fang said. "But what has this to do with Opal?"

"Oh, I think the two of them seemed *close* at one time," Little Jade said, biting on her handkerchief. She lowered her voice to a whisper. "Master Jiang-Min got tired of Opal for a while—he had a new concubine from the South—and Opal got involved with Yao. I think Yao had liked her for a long time, but couldn't make his move because Master Jiang-Min had claimed her. Well, Opal was seen a lot with him, but after Yao turned violent, she made it clear that she didn't want anything to do with him anymore. I believe she asked our mistress to find a matchmaker so she could be married off quickly. I don't blame her a bit; Yao was quite capable of murder." Then her eyes widened when she said the word *murder*.

Fang was also thinking the same thing. If Yao and Opal had been an item and the girl eventually left him, it was quite possible that Yao had hunted her down and killed her in a fit of rage and jealousy.

"You said he once worked here," Fang said, looking her directly in the eye. "Where is he now?"

"I think the last I heard of him, he became a professional wrestler," Little Jade said. "With his strength and skill, he'd make more money collecting winnings than doing heavy labour. But I don't know where you can find him."

"I thank you for your help, Little Jade." Fang removed a small jade pendant from his girdle and handed it to her. "Here—this should be worth five taels of silver. Buy some pretty things with it."

The girl's eyes shone. "Oh, you don't have to, I'd do anything if it'd help Opal." Her fingers closed around the pendant, however.

78

Fang took his leave, satisfied with the information so far. Since he had Yao's full name, it should not be difficult to find the man. A small part of him felt sorry for Chow. It must come as a shock that your beloved was concealing secrets from you— first the debt, and now two past lovers.

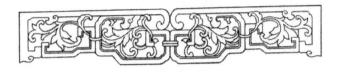

10

Hong made her way to Family Luo's, a winehouse that advertised itself as "Best Wine Under Heaven." Since Shue's birthday banquet, the wine cellar had been depleted, and Shue had requested she go to Mr. Luo's and place a new order for fifty jars of Rose Daughter, which was the winehouse's most popular brand.

The winehouse owner was pleased to see her, and even offered her a sample. Hong declined; she had never been a good drinker, but she thanked him courteously. Many owners or managers treated her as a servant—well, she was, but she disliked being ordered around in a blunt, rude manner. Sometimes when the men made lewd jokes, she could only bow her head and silently wish she could shoot darts into their most precious body parts. If someone tried to make a grab at her, she'd evade with precise and deft skill.

Fortunately, she did not have to come to this part of town frequently, and with experience she had learnt to make herself as inconspicuous as possible, which was not as difficult as it might seem. Without the glamorous costumes and makeup, she looked plain enough—few heads turned when she walked by. Plus, being meticulously neat and clear-eyed marked her as a girl of a respectable household, not some poor girl who could be easily taken advantage of.

When she left the winehouse, Hong was feeling rather hungry. She walked up and down the street, until the aroma of meat buns arrested her. She bought a couple of buns and stood near the entrance of a narrow alley, eating slowly.

Suddenly, she thought she saw Fang go by. She stepped a bit further out of the alley, and sure enough, it was him dressed in a simple granite-coloured robe.

What was Fang doing here? The direction he was heading was towards the Willow Quarters—a street lined with brothels. Having grown up with Fang, she knew that he never visited brothels—at least not that she knew of. It was natural that he would want to take care of his primal needs, but it was strange that he would choose to pay for a prostitute, who might carry a sexual disease, when he could easily have bedded one of the maidservants at home. While he was not the eldest son, who carried the biggest privilege, Fang was nevertheless young and handsome, not to mention accomplished in sports and music. Hong knew that many maids would have gladly spent a night with him without even demanding to be made his concubine thereafter.

Or perhaps he wasn't going for the sexual experience. There were a number of high-class courtesans in the area, whose beauty and talent would rival even an aristocrat's daughter. Maybe one of his brothers had passed on a recommendation. Still, Hong couldn't fathom why Fang would be heading to the brothel alone, and moreover, so plainly dressed, as though he wanted to stay anonymous.

She slipped into the street, making sure to keep a considerable distance between Fang and herself. Plenty of people on the streets offered enough camouflage. A couple of men leered at her, but she avoided eye contact and put on a blank, formidable expression, walking with a confidence and firmness in her step. Were anyone to bother her, she could discreetly toss a small stone that would hit a pressure point. Any normal person unschooled in martial arts would double up in pain.

Fang made his way to the back of a large building with red lanterns hanging in front. Hong knew the place; it was the largest brothel in town, Heavenly Pleasures. She had finished off a few particularly cruel and vicious people here.

Hong watched as he walked briskly to the back entrance. A few prostitutes leered at him; one tried to take his arm, but Fang shook his head. When she complained, he removed her hand firmly and talked to another prostitute.

Thanks to her exceptional hearing under the tutelage of Old Man Liu, Hong caught what he was saying: "Tell your mistress that the governor's son has arrived on business."

It didn't make sense. What would Fang have to do with the owner of a brothel?

There was a movement near her, and Hong quickly ducked behind a thick bush. A couple of male servants staggered past, singing ribald songs.

If she wanted to find out what Fang was up to, she had to go in disguise. Her clothing was too clean and fine to be a brothel servant's, nor was it bright and revealing enough to be a prostitute's.

Hong waited for her chance. However, there were too many people passing by the back door. Since she had visited the brothel before, Hong knew there was one side where fewer people went by.

She slipped quietly around the corner, where there was an alley so narrow that only one or two people could squeeze by. She unwound the scarf she wore wrapped round her sleeves, extracted a pair of bamboo hooks from her pouch, and attached the hooks to the end of the scarf. Then she threw the scarf into the air; the hooks fitted neatly on the window sill.

Taking a deep breath, she leaped into the air. One foot hit the wall for support; her next leap brought her right over the window.

Immediately, she encountered a servant girl carrying a pot of wine. The girl let out a small shriek and dropped the wine.

Like an arrow, Hong shot out and caught the pot deftly with her left hand. At the same time, her right arm came up and her elbow hit the girl's chin smartly, knocking her out.

Hong uttered a silent apology, hoping that the girl hadn't suffered too much pain. She listened carefully for a few seconds, trying to determine which room was completely devoid of human activity, then dragged the unconscious girl into an empty room. To ensure that she would not wake up too soon, Hong hit a couple of pressure points on the girl's shoulder blades and her waist. It would take a few hours before she awoke.

Hong hid the girl behind the door, along with the pot of wine. Her original plan was to change clothes with the girl, but a quick glance told her it was not feasible. First, the girl was much shorter than her; Hong did not want her skirt riding up her legs. Second, she would have to return to retrieve her own clothes; no way could she return to the governor's compound dressed like a prostitute.

But she had to act fast, or she'd miss Fang's meeting with the brothel owner. Hong bit her lip and removed her upper robe, revealing her bare shoulders. She tugged her lower robe a bit lower so it showed cleavage, and made sure her sash was tied securely around her midriff. Then she took the servant girl's shawl—it was semi-transparent, as current fashion dictated—and pulled it over her shoulders.

Even with the shawl, she felt uncomfortable and exposed, but it was no time to be self-conscious. She couldn't leave her upper robe behind, so Hong uncorked the pot of wine and let a good amount of wine spill over the robe. Tucking the soiled robe under her arm, she opened the door and slipped into the corridor.

Since she had been to Heavenly Pleasures for a mission just three months earlier, Hong knew the layout of the building fairly well. She remembered that the owner, Madam Jin, occupied the top floor, where she held secret meetings with a few lovers and discussed important matters with prospective clients.

Hong hurried to the stairs, keeping her head down. Fortunately, since it was still early morning, few guests loitered around. Indeed, the place was mostly quiet except for snores from late risers and quick footsteps from servants carrying breakfast and cleaning supplies.

On the landing of the top floor, Hong paused for a second. Voices belonging to Fang and Madam Jin drifted from the room in the end of the corridor. Noiselessly, Hong crept towards the room, which was of course closed (and most likely locked), and looked around for a place to hide.

The heavy wooden rafters on the ceiling looked sturdy enough. Hong used her inner force to leap onto the rafters and settle her weight on a thick beam. Unless someone on the corridor made a point to look up, she would not be discovered.

"… very punctual, my dear young man," Madam Jin was purring.

She heard the rustling of thick, crisp paper. "Here," Fang said tonelessly. "The remaining amount. Five sheets, a hundred taels each."

"Such a good friend you are." Madam Jin let out a high-pitched laugh. Hong felt like stuffing her ears, but reminded herself she was here to eavesdrop. Why was Fang handing over so much money to the brothel owner? Even the Queen of Flowers, the most famous and expensive courtesan, at Heavenly Pleasures should not cost more than three hundred taels, unless Fang was bidding for her first night. And why had Madam Jin complimented him for being a good friend? Who was she referring to?

A rustle of silk and the tinkling of jade pieces hitting together came from the stairs.

The most beautiful woman Hong had ever seen appeared. She barely wore any makeup, but she still was incredibly attractive. Skin as white as the most delicate porcelain, eyes like pools of black lagoons, lips as luscious as the litchi fruit ripe and fresh from its peel. Ebony hair, long and luxuriant and shiny, cascaded down her robes in rich waves.

And not only were her features stunning, she moved with a grace like running water. She walked— no, glided—over the polished wooden floor with smooth, fluid steps. Her fancy robes—layers and layers of high-quality silk—billowed behind her as though she were flying. Hong instinctively knew that this perfect creature must also be an accomplished dancer.

The woman stopped outside Madam Jin's door. Hong snapped her attention back to Fang and Jin and chided herself. In the temporary moment of being awestruck by the newcomer, she had lost whatever conversation went between Fang and Jin.

"... have no idea what you are talking about, but I've never heard the girl mention him. You'd best be asking the people at Duel of Death."

"All right. In that case, I bid you good day, madam."

"Wait!" The older woman raised her voice. "Are you simply going to leave?"

Silence. Hong wished that she could see Fang's expression.

"But this is Heavenly Pleasures, my dear young man. Surely you didn't come with the sole purpose of paying off your friend's debt! Are you training to be a monk?"

Hong gripped the rafters tightly, so hard that she didn't notice a splinter cutting into her skin. Which of Fang's friends was in debt?

"No." Fang's voice remained curt. Hong reflected on how seldom she'd heard him use that tone with her. He reserved it only for people he detested, yet didn't wish to be rude to.

Fang opened the door. His hand paused on the frame when he beheld the lovely courtesan standing outside. She seemed also surprised that he had suddenly emerged, but immediately sank into a graceful curtsy, her silken skirts rustling on the floor, and glanced up at him through long fringed eyelashes.

Hong closed her eyes briefly. She shouldn't have done that, really, she should focus her entire attention on them, but just for that moment, she didn't want to look at Fang and see him fall head over heels for another.

"Moon Fairy!" Madam Jin's shrill voice echoed through the corridor. "Just in time, I've been thinking of you! This is Master Shue Fang, one of the governor's sons!"

Fang winced. He gave Moon Fairy a short bow and prepared to leave.

"Wait!" Madam Jin suddenly caught his sleeve and pulled him back. "Didn't you say you're seeking a man called Yao? Well, one of our frequent guests is currently working at Duel of Death. Moon Fairy, why don't you show him where Mr. Liang is resting?"

Moon Fairy smiled—a smile that could make men empty their money bags. "It'd be my pleasure, Master Fang."

Fang turned a deep shade of red. "I don't think…"

"Not everyone can meet Invincible Yao, young man," Madam Jin said. "Mr. Liang, as the manager of Duel of Death, can help you. It's unlikely he will refuse your request while his head is still thick from fine wine and carnal pleasure."

Moon Fairy moved closer and touched his arm. "It will not take long, Master Fang. Mr. Liang occupies a room just a floor below."

Fang swallowed. "Lead the way."

Moon Fairy curtsied deeply. She swept away as though walking on clouds; Fang stood still for a second before following her. Madam Jin looked after them, a satisfied smirk pasted on her large, pear-shaped face.

There was nothing more Hong wanted than to slip down from her hiding place and see what business Fang had with Mr. Liang. She knew well that Liang was no good man, from reports of his decadent life as manager of the largest fight arena in the city, though he hadn't done anything that warranted a death sentence. Still, nothing good could come from Fang meeting him. And why was Fang seeking Invincible Yao? From what she had heard, Yao was the star fighter of Duel of Death. Surely Fang was not seeking him for a duel?

While she was thus preoccupied with questions, her right foot slipped from the beam.

Madam Jin, who was still standing in the corridor, looked up.

Hong quickly flattened herself on the beam, praying that the thickness of the wooden construction was sufficient to shield her from view. Her heart beat wildly.

It seemed an eternity until Madam Jin turned back. She moved to stand in front of the railings and looked down. From her location, she could see Moon Fairy leading Fang to Mr. Liang's room.

Hong grit her teeth as she watched the older woman's fat fingers tap on the ebony railings. A big ruby ring glowed on her thumb.

"Hmph." Madam Jin made a low snort which sounded like disapproval. "Refusing an invitation to stay, eh? Idiot."

Hong craned her neck as much as she deemed safe. Dimly, she thought she could see the pale pink robe of Moon Fairy, who was on the floor below, but not the granite colour of Fang's robe. Either he was in another room or had departed. Judging from Madam Jin's snort, she guessed it should be the latter.

Relieved, Hong allowed herself to smile.

The rest of the eavesdropping went poorly, however. Madam Jin waited until Moon Fairy returned and scolded her for failing to engage the governor's son for a morning repast.

"Have you forgotten what I've taught you?" she hissed. "Did you try leaning down and letting your cleavage show? Did you let your hair brush over his sleeve? Or even pretending to faint—even a man made of iron couldn't just let you fall!"

Moon Fairy bowed low; her beautiful face was contrite.

"Mother, I am sorry. But he had no intention of dallying…"

"Fool!" Madam Jin raised her hand as though to strike her face, but stopped. It would be unwise to mar the girl's beauty. Instead, she caught Moon Fairy's shoulders and gave her a shake. "If you had truly made an effort to seduce him, no man could resist you! If only he had stayed, we could have told General Su that we have the governor's son competing for your hand, and he would have raised his price on you!"

"Sorry, Mother. Next time I will do better."

"Highly unlikely there'll be a next time," Madam Jin huffed. "I know he isn't the kind to seek pleasure on his own. Go back to your room and repent on your half-hearted behaviour. Remember, if you want to fetch a high price when you are finally married off, you *need* to attract as much competition as possible. Let your suitors know that you are hard to get." She pointed a fat finger at Moon Fairy, the rubies on her hand glittering. "Don't disappoint me, girl. I worked hard to bring you up to be the Queen of Flowers."

She waddled off, her leather shoes creaking on the wooden floor. Moon Fairy sank on the floor and buried her face in her hands.

Hong felt a strong rush of sympathy. Just a while ago, she had resented the courtesan's impact on Fang, but now she actually wished that Fang had showed a bit more attention.

Fang. He probably had already left the place. Hong waited until Moon Fairy left, then slipped down the rafters. Her mind brimming with questions, she made her way back to the governor's compound.

She longed to ask Fang what on earth he was doing, but she couldn't ask without giving away herself. What would he say if he learnt she had been to Heavenly Pleasures? What would he think if he knew her first kill had been disposing of a sadistic patron at the brothel?

Since she had been gone for some time, Hong decided to make some purchases at the market to account for her absence. Not only could you purchase fresh produce and meat, but also imported goods from the Persians, Uighurs, Turks, Japanese and Koreans. You could have your fortune told, your portrait painted, and for those who were illiterate, there were even calligraphers who would write letters by dictation. Besides rows and rows of stalls, hawkers and peddlers plodded on, balancing bamboo yokes over their shoulders.

When she passed the market, Hong was surprised to see Shu-Mo, Fang's personal servant, dictating something at a calligrapher's stall. The calligrapher's ink brush moved deftly over a scroll of snowy white paper; even at a distance, Hong could tell from his movements that the man was skilled.

Perhaps she could wheedle something out of the lad; Fang treated Shu-Mo more like a friend than servant.

"Hello," Hong said.

Shu-Mo jumped three feet in the air. "Miss Hong! Wha... what are you doing here?"

"I was going to ask you the same thing." Hong nodded towards the calligrapher. "Are you up to something secret that not even your master knows?"

The lad turned bright red. "It's nothing."

Hong quirked an eyebrow. She knew that Shu-Mo was literate—and also stingy. If he was willing to spend coppers to pay for an expert to write for him, it couldn't be something easily dismissed. A love letter, most likely.

"By the way, have you seen Young Master Fang?" Hong decided not to tease him further. After all, her purpose was to enquire after Fang's reason for visiting Heavenly Pleasures.

Shu-Mo immediately shook his head. "N… no. I haven't seen him. At all." But his eyes were darting back and forth. Judging from his friendship with Fang, it was more possible that the young master had told him not to tell anyone that he was going to the brothel.

Hong pondered on how to question him further without making things too difficult for him, but just then, someone tugged on her sleeve.

It was Ah-Ming.

"Mr. Liu wants to see me?" Hong asked.

Ah-Ming nodded.

Well… it looked like she would have to find some other opportunity to learn about Fang's doings.

She bade Shu-Mo goodbye, the latter clearly relieved.

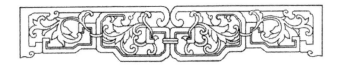

11

On the way to the apothecary, Hong noticed that Ah-Ming was quieter than usual. He was not a talkative child, but he usually would greet her with a bashful smile. Today, he kept his face down and did not look at her. It looked as though a dark cloud was hovering over him.

"Are you feeling well today?" Hong tried to touch his forehead, but the boy pushed her hand away and shook his head.

Today certainly was full of strange things. First Fang visited a brothel but not for pleasure, and now Ah-Ming was not talking to her.

At the drug store, Meng-Ting was weighing a bunch of lotus roots on bronze scales.

"There you are." Meng-Ting wrapped the lotus roots in a piece of oiled paper. "Ah-Ming, would you like to help me put away these herbs?"

Ah-Ming nodded and shuffled to the back of the house. His back was hunched over, adding to his dejected look.

"Has anything happened to him?" she asked in a low voice. "He seems so... low-spirited."

Meng-Ting sighed. A brief look of pain crossed his face. "You'll hear from Grandfather later."

Hong wasn't quite sure why Old Man Liu had something to do with Ah-Ming's mood, but she did not question further. "You sent Ah-Ming to find me."

A customer happened to drop by at the moment. "Doctor Liu! My back has been aching all day long! Have you a lotion that can cure sore backs?"

"Right away, Mrs. Yang." Meng-Ting rummaged in the drawers and withdrew a package. "Rub this on your back three times a day. If it doesn't work, come back and I'll give you another for free."

"Thank you. Mind if I sit in front of your shop for a moment? Been carrying buckets of water the whole morning."

"Of course, of course." Meng-Ting brought out a low stool and set it on the ground. "You deserve a rest after all the hard work you've been doing."

Mrs. Yang plopped on the stool with a grin. Drawing a large floppy fan woven from reeds, she began to fan herself noisily, letting out a sigh every ten seconds.

Meng-Ting and Hong exchanged a look. Mrs. Yang was known to be one of the biggest gossips in the city.

"Grandfather wants to hear how you've been practising that new song," Meng-Ting said lightly, in the same tone as if he were chatting about the weather. "He says that you need to work harder on your flute playing."

Hong pretended to sigh. "*Sifu* is so demanding. I believe I didn't perform badly at Master Shue's banquet, but still he isn't satisfied."

"You know Grandfather's always like that. Probably it's more likely he wants your company than to criticise your ability." Meng-Ting gave a good-natured shrug. "And give him some of this tea, a friend of mine brought it from the South. Very refreshing, and the scent isn't too strong. Best on the second steeping, but since it's expensive, you can drink the first cup and give my grandfather the second."

"Will do." Hong tucked the bag of tea in her girdle. "Do you mind if I also request some of that rouge you gave me last time? I believe my supply is running short. The maids keep complimenting your products; Golden Lotus made off with an entire jar." She was lying deliberately. Meng-Ting knew nothing about making cosmetics.

Meng-Ting nodded knowingly. "Ah, I had no idea my little hobby was so popular. Wish it was my winning personality rather than my rouge." He disappeared into another room and soon emerged with a small pouch of bright red silk. "This contains my latest concoction. I've written up the instructions, in case you might forget. The effects, I believe, are better than the lotion I gave you last time. Hope it will come to good use soon."

Hong thanked him and secured the pouch in her bosom pocket. Both of them knew well that whenever she asked for a "beauty product," it actually meant that she needed more poison or drugs.

When she reached Old Man Liu's compound, the door wasn't bolted so she went straight in. Liu was not in the courtyard, nor was he in the compound. Hong paused in one of the rooms and listened. She thought she heard faint sounds of needles cutting through the air, so she walked towards the northeast of the compound, where a small gate led to a clump of tall maple trees outside.

Old Man Liu was sitting on a large rock, his right hand holding a bunch of needles. There was a breeze in the air, lifting the strands of his greying hair and making the ends of his long sleeves flutter. A stronger gust of wind came up, bringing a shower of large maple leaves down to the ground. Before the leaves hit the earth, however, Liu raised his hand.

Gleams of silver flashed in the swirl of yellow and red. Hong squinted; a dozen or so maple leaves were pinned to the tree trunk by Liu's silver needles.

"Retrieve the needles." Old Man Liu spoke without even looking at her.

Hong was already moving towards the tree. She couldn't help but marvel how her *sifu* had managed to catch the falling leaves while relying on his hearing alone. Could she do the same with her eyes blindfolded?

As if reading her thoughts, Liu said, "Take the needles and come here. When the next wind arises, close your eyes and let the needles fly."

Hong obeyed.

Her first couple tries were dismal. Just one or two maple leaves were pinned successfully to the tree. Her past training had sharpened her eyesight and hearing, but she had yet to try aiming in complete darkness. She still had a long way to go before she could emulate her *sifu*. Were Meng-Ting present, he might have tried cheating by keeping his eyes open, but Hong did not bother. She respected her *sifu* too much.

"Don't be impatient, girl," Liu growled. "Listen with your soul, as you do with music."

"Yes, *sifu*."

Hong took a deep breath and relaxed her shoulders. This time, she tried not to think at all—not to let her determination to succeed occupy her head. Instead, she cleared all thoughts from her mind and just let herself soak up the surroundings. Around her, she could feel the coolness of autumn air against her skin, smell the crispness of the leaves, and gradually, every tiny nuance of movement seemed to be within hearing. It was as if she were no longer human, she was now part of nature.

Then the wind came.

She raised her hand, almost by pure instinct. She could hear the faintest crackle and rustle of the maple leaves, could *feel* the wind currents running around the leaves, bringing them down...

The needles burst from her fingers and whipped through the air. When she heard the tiny thuds of needles hitting the trunk, she knew she had done better.

Hong opened her eyes. But even before she could count the maple leaves, her *sifu* spoke.

"Eight. I see you have grasped the principle, girl."

Hong couldn't help feeling a small elation from a sense of achievement.

"Thank you, *sifu*."

She remained standing where she was, however. Surely her *sifu* had not asked Meng-Ting to send for her just to introduce a new training method. There must be something more.

"I have another mission for you," Old Man Liu said. "This one will be more difficult than the corrupt officers and lecherous merchants you used to dispose of. He is a well-trained fighter of hand-to-hand combat, and his martial abilities are said to be the best in the city. However, with the new drug Meng-Ting has concocted and the improvement of your skills, you should be able to take care of him without too much difficulty."

Hong brushed off a small leaf that had fallen on her shoulder. "May I enquire the fighter you speak of?"

"Yao. He's currently the star fighter at Duel of Death."

12

"According to our sources," Old Man Liu said, twirling a needle between his fingers, "Yao was a bodyguard who worked for the magistrate. A very capable fighter he was, being tall and muscular, and he trained in the Shaolin School for Non-Religious People, which means of course that he received the best martial arts education. However, he became dangerous when he took up drinking. The magistrate had to dismiss him when he killed a harmless old servant in a fit of drunken rage."

"So where is Yao now?" Hong said.

"He took on some odd jobs, but eventually ended up as a professional wrestler at Duel of Death. He takes a good percentage for every fight he wins—and it's said he lost only once in the two-hundred-odd games he's participated in! Not a bad job—better than brick-laying or cattle-keeping, anyway. Of course, for the true martial artist, selling your skills in a brawl is not respectable. But does Yao care? From what I've heard, he *revels* in beating up his opponents. Killed one of them, too."

Hong looked down at her hands. She had never been assigned to kill a fighter, and from the picture Liu was painting, it'd be a tasteless job. Could she really succeed? In the past, she had managed to kill easily because the opponents knew nothing about martial arts, but against a professional fighter who had lost only once?

"If it's just killing in the profession, then we wouldn't be bothered," Old Man Liu said. "Injuries happen to the wrestling folks every day. They even have to sign a life-death sheet before plunging into battle—you know, a testimony that no matter what happens in the arena, the loser or his family will not seek revenge. But girlie, Yao has killed innocent people. That young boy Meng-Ting employed—Ah-Ming is his name, eh? Yao got drunk a few days ago and knocked over a noodle shop by the street. Hot noodle soup splashed all over him."

Hong's eyes widened.

"Turns out the noodle shop owner is Ah-Ming's father. Yao was furious when he was scalded by the soup. Got into a quarrel with the poor man, and in the end, Yao gave him a blow that cracked his ribs. And he didn't stop. The witnesses said that Yao kept on hitting him, blow after blow, until the man crumpled up in a puddle of his own blood."

Hong clenched her fists. "Nothing was done?"

"The people at Duel of Death covered up the best they could. They're rolling in dough—the arena is always fully packed, and the managers also run the biggest gambling house in town. They threatened the few witnesses and told them not to let the matter reach the magistrate—though even if it did, I don't think it'll make any difference. Magistrate Ho is just as corrupted and weak as any official at court. Gift him a chest filled with gold and he'll lick the dirt off your shoes."

"What about Ah-Ming's family?"

"There's only the old grandmother left. She couldn't do anything, not even complain. Meng-Ting reported to me that Manager Liang, along with three brawny minions, visited the house and told her to keep quiet or her grandson will be in trouble. So what can the grandmother do but shut her mouth and bury her son? She had to beg from the neighbours to pool together enough coppers for a reed mat and hire help to dig the grave. Meng-Ting also shared the expense when he learnt about it, or Ah-Ming would have to find labour work to pay for it. He's only ten, girlie!"

Even Old Man Liu, gruff and irascible, sounded cracked when he spoke.

Hong silently wiped a tear. She couldn't believe it was only a few days ago that she sat down to a bowl of noodle soup at Ah-Ming's father's shop. The poor child. No wonder he had looked so depressed.

"This has to be stopped," she found herself saying.

Old Man Liu cleared his throat. "I've planned it out for you, girlie. The next wrestling match will be tomorrow night. Tell your master that I require your presence, but go to Meng-Ting's first. He'll provide you with a disguise. You shall dress up as a man, enter Duel of Death, and find a chance to poison Yao. Meng-Ting should have given you the poison already—yes, that's the bottle. The poison will not work immediately; it takes effect best when one is

101

exercising and the blood runs fast in one's veins. Let Yao die in the fighting ring—preferably by the hand of his opponent. Make sure your disguise is flawless so no one will suspect you!"

Hong bowed her head. "It shall be done, *sifu.*"

Back at the governor's compound, Fang paced the floor in his room. Shu-Mo sat cross-legged in a corner, polishing the sheath of Fang's dagger.

"So how did it go at the brothel?" Shu-Mo said.

"Not bad." Fang ran a hand through his hair. "Chow's debts are taken care of. Also, I met Mr. Liang. He's the owner of Duel of Death, and he promised to let me meet Yao. Yao has a fight with a martial artist from the South tomorrow night."

"That simple? Liang knows that you suspect Yao has murdered Opal, yet he readily agrees to give you Yao's address?"

"I was surprised as well," Fang said slowly. "He probably thinks I'm no threat. Yao has a nickname of Invincible. Besides…" He stopped, not wanting to mention that Moon Fairy had taken Liang's arm and urged him to say yes. That courtesan was simply irresistible. It had taken Fang a good amount of willpower not to accept her invitation for a cup of wine. Even though she clearly manifested an interest in him, it simply wasn't in his nature to court another, not when he was still hopelessly in love with Hong.

"Besides what?" Shu-Mo asked curiously.

"Nothing. No matter what, I should go to Yao's house tomorrow to find out. It's quite likely that he murdered Chow's wife due to a fit of jealousy."

"I don't like the idea of confronting someone from Duel of Death," Shu-Mo said, as he sharpened Fang's sword on the grindstone. "Maybe the girl committed suicide because she didn't want to be burdened with those debts anymore. Or maybe... here's a thought. Maybe *Chow* killed his wife because he discovered her liaison with Yao!"

"Hold your tongue," Fang said sharply. "Chow isn't that kind of person. We have no proof that Opal was carrying on an affair behind his back—she only concealed her debts from her husband. Why would she continue her affair with a man who has clearly displayed a violent nature?"

"Oh, some women are idiots," Shu-Mo said, shaking his head. "Young Master, you remember the laundry lady? She got a blackened eye *again* from her abusive husband, but she doesn't want to leave him. Golden Lotus said she only vowed a few weeks ago she would never take him back after what he did to her, but all it takes is a few pretty words and a bowed head, and she believes that things will be changed for the better."

"My friend is no murderer," Fang reiterated. "Tomorrow we will seek Yao and make him confess."

Shu-Mo had an expression that said he didn't approve, but he resumed his sharpening more vigorously. "By the way, Hong was asking where you went this morning."

Fang stopped his pacing. "She was asking for me?"

"She saw me at the market, where I was—er—she saw me anyway, and I guess she found it weird that you weren't around. So she asked where you were."

"Only that? She didn't say anything about maybe seeing me later?"

"I'm afraid not, Young Master." Seeing that Fang looked disappointed, Shu-Mo hastily added, "But she didn't just walk away. A boy came to find her—I think it was the boy from Mr. Liu, the apothecary—so she had to leave."

His attempt to comfort his master failed, especially when he mentioned Meng-Ting. Fang scowled. What kind of business was Liu Meng-Ting bothering Hong for? She was a musician, not a physician.

"Well, let's hope things will go well tomorrow," Fang said, deciding he would seek Hong later. Once this matter of Opal was taken care of, he would commence seriously his pursuit of Hong. He had always wanted her, and he was not going to give up without   trying.

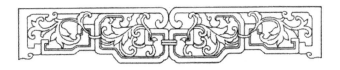

13

Hong touched her hair self-consciously when she stopped in front of Duel of Death, making sure it was securely bound in her cloth cap. Even though men also wore their hair down, her features would look more feminine if her hair escaped from its high knot and tumbled around her face, and thus it would be easier to discover she was a woman. Not that cross-dressing was a complete novelty. Hong had seen women dressing up as men and partaking in masculine pursuits—even in wrestling—but the more distance she could put between her and her identity as the governor's maidservant, the better.

She was dressed in long, baggy trousers and a tunic the colour of dull grey (no female at the Shue household would be caught wearing that colour), her hair completely tied up in a bun. She did have makeup smeared over her face, but it was a yellow-brownish substance Meng-Ting had provided, so her skin would look darker and thus more weather-battered.

Hong gritted her teeth, remembering how Meng-Ting had fussed over her just a while ago, when he was getting her ready for the masquerade.

"Throw back your shoulders when you walk, Hong," Meng-Ting had said. "Heavens, when was the last time Grandfather had you masquerade as a man? You have to act less refined! How about clearing your throat and spitting?"

"Cannot I pretend to be a scholar instead?" Hong had asked, tugging at her sash with frustration. Her figure was not curvy, but the breast bands felt so restrictive. She was more at ease with posing as a well-bred lady or a courtesan.

"Scholars don't frequent wrestling rings," Meng-Ting had said. "Well, perhaps a few do, but you'd better be prepared to offer a damned good reason. You know, the scholars who also practise with a sword because they think it looks fashionable—their skills are showy and lack substance. *Real* fighting is brutal and ugly, and thank heavens I'm not forced to partake in anything like it."

"It doesn't make you less intimidating," Hong said, holding up a needle tip that had been submerged in poison for several hours. "You can still kill... and be a lot stealthier."

"I'm a physician!" Meng-Ting insisted. "I heal rather than harm. But if I had the chance—I'd run a knife through that Yao if I could. Ah-Ming has stopped speaking completely, you know? I've been trying to get him to open up—I haven't even seen the child cry, he's hurting too much inside. All I can do now is send food baskets to his grandmother, who's begging me to keep things quiet. She lost her son already, she doesn't want to lose another loved one."

"Understandable." Hong fitted a dagger in her boot. "But if we don't stop him now, there's no telling when Yao will go into another drunken rage. No more innocent lives should be sacrificed."

Hong scanned the fight arena ahead. She had never been here before, though Old Man Liu had mentioned she should visit some time. She could learn a thing from observing how others fight, even though the fights at Duel of Death were not "real." Despite its ominous name, fighting to the death was not received favourably. People paid to see a satisfying battle, to see fighters pushed to the verge of death but *not* actually dying.

There was a deafening roar from the crowd inside. Maybe a winner was being announced.

Hong wondered if Yao was already in battle. As the best wrestler in the place, he would not be fighting so early. He would probably be located in a special room somewhere, getting ready for final domination.

When she tried to enter, two burly men stopped her at the door.

"Admission fee," one growled.

Hong hesitated, wondering if she had enough on her.

"You look like a greenie," the other said, staring at her face. "Never been here before?"

Hong nodded.

"Two strings of copper, then," the man said. "We're cutting you some slack. And make it quick, we haven't all day."

She had exactly three strings of copper with her. Hong sighed inwardly and dug out the money. Not that she needed a lot to spend, but two strings of copper was easily a week's wages for a poor family. How easy it was for people to gamble away their hard-earned money!

Once she was allowed entrance, Hong scanned the interior. A sturdy wooden stage had been erected in the middle of a huge courtyard. The audience, mostly men, gathered around the stage, their attention riveted on the two wrestlers fighting on top.

In the back of the stage was a long house guarded by a dozen heavyset men, all of them armed with various weapons from swords to whips. One had a row of throwing knives displayed openly on his sleeve. Hong wondered how accurate his aim was.

She couldn't resist a peek at the stage. One wrestler was large and bulky, yet he moved surprisingly fast for a man of his size. The other wrestler was tall and lean, and his moves were fluid and poised, as though he had choreographed his fight routine. Both of them wore their hair in a tight ponytail, their torsos bare and slick with sweat.

Suddenly, the large man lunged forward, attempting to catch the tall man's ankles. His opponent, quick to sense the attack, reacted by aiming a powerful kick at the large man's forehead.

Wrong move.

Snap.

The large man brought his hands together, trapping the tall man's foot between his hands. With a deft twist, he dislocated the ankle joint, causing the tall man to gasp in pain. Using the precious few seconds, the large man caught the tall man's waist, lifted him in the air, and dumped him unceremoniously on the ground. Bones cracked when the tall man hit the floor.

The winner was obvious.

Below, the commotion was thunderous. Those who had staked their money on the large man were roaring with glee, while those who had had faith in the tall man looked sullen and frustrated. Several assistants leaped on the stage and started to escort the tall man off the stage.

"Damn." A man near her balled his fists. "Half my savings gone! Who'd have known that oaf would win? Damn!"

Hong sidled up to him. "Brother, perhaps you'd have better luck laying your odds on Yao the Invincible instead? I heard it's a sure bet."

"No surprises with Yao, the stakes are pretty low," the man grumbled. "He only lost once! Unless they bring a three-headed, six-armed man in here, I wouldn't think of laying odds against him."

"When will Yao be up?" Hong asked. "I've been hoping to see him fight up close; I'd better push through the crowds fast if I want to see him."

"Oh, he wouldn't be up for another hour," the man said, waving her off. "He's the reigning champion, they always save him for last. Are you planning to stake all your pitiful earnings on him, young one? I'd warn you that the winnings won't be as much as you think!"

"I see," Hong said, pretending to look disappointed. "Oh well, I suppose I shall have to content myself with watching him fight. A man named Invincible would be worth watching alone!"

"Ain't it so?" the man said, giving her a slap on the back. Remembering what Meng-Ting advised,

Hong returned the gesture with a clap on the shoulder. "First time here, eh? Don't let your jaw fall on the ground!"

Hong grinned. "Well, in that case I'll take a small break. Save a place for me, would you?"

"Going to relieve yourself?" The man gave a raucous laugh. "Yeah, don't want to wet yourself if things get rough, huh?"

Hong managed a short laugh in response and turned away.

Once she had squeezed her way out of the crowd, doing her best to tolerate the smell of dirt and sweat, she scanned for the wounded tall man, who was being carried off the stage. A bald man shouted directions for the tall man to be carried upstairs.

Hong reached into her long sleeve and felt for her needles, which were packed securely in a tiny pouch. These were specially made of glass, so they were practically invisible when flashing through the air, their length not exceeding her little finger. Each of them was dipped in poison, courtesy of Meng-Ting.

The plan was simple—once Yao was on stage, she would loosen a needle and let it enter Yao's body. She would make sure to aim for the thigh, where the flesh was plentiful and so that none of the glass end would be visible. Each needle was dipped in the poison Meng-Ting slipped for her, right under Mrs. Yang's nose. The poison would take effect within seconds—when Yao was deep in a fight, his blood circulation would ensure that the poison would spread rapidly through his body, causing a numbness. His opponent, unknowingly, would be able to land a couple powerful blows. Yao would be beaten to death;

even if he were only seriously injured, the poison would ensure he die afterwards.

The trick, however, was that she had to be close enough to the stage to take aim. Her glass needles were so tiny that they couldn't reach a long distance, and besides, she didn't want to accidentally harm anyone standing in front of her.

Making sure that she had everything ready, Hong hurried back to the crowd, pushing her way to the front. The smell of sweat and wine and bad breath made her want to hold her nose, the dirty clothes and clammy skin from some bare arms made her want to shrink back, but she kept going. Luckily, few people bothered her except for a couple disgruntled looks.

"All right, folks!" the co-manager called. He was a corpulent man whose lungs certainly granted him extra volume. "Next up is Mighty Bull from Chang-an, against a wandering swordswoman, Flying Swallow!"

A middle-aged man with powerful, log-like arms leaped on the stage, followed by a slender young woman. Although the woman was average-looking and conservatively dressed in grey robes, her hair concealed entirely in a grey cloth cap, several men in the audience started whistling and calling out lecherous comments. The woman, however, maintained a calm demeanour, as though she were meditating in the mountains instead of standing in a fight arena.

"Let the match begin!"

With a roar that echoed through the ceiling, Mighty Bull hit out with his huge hands, aiming for the abdomen. The audience held their breath; once hit by his tremendous strength, Flying Swallow would be dead on the spot. Her only chance was to dodge, though such a choice might lead to her falling off the stage.

But contrary to expectations, she didn't jump away. Her feet firmly pinned on the ground, Flying Swallow leaned backwards, her upper torso only a hand's breadth from the ground. Mighty Bull's attack met thin air.

A murmur of awe ran through the crowd. Even Hong was impressed by the woman's flexibility.

But Flying Swallow didn't just evade the attack. She planted her elbows firmly on the ground, supporting her weight, and raised her right leg instead, kicking out at Mighty Bull.

Bam!

Her foot struck Mighty Bull smartly on the throat. Strong as the Chang-an fighter might be, there was no way he could train his throat to be as solid and hard as his torso. Even though Flying Swallow's kick was not bone-shattering, it was enough to make him grunt in pain.

By now, those who had laid their odds against Flying Swallow looked crestfallen. In a match when the fighters could only rely on fists, women were usually at a disadvantage. Who'd have expected the young woman to be such a contender?

Hong was fascinated. No wonder Duel of Death was so popular; violent as it was, the show was truly captivating. Since Flying Swallow had a body build similar to hers, Hong could learn a few things about fighting to her advantage, simply by observing how the young woman bested a man almost twice her size.

A few minutes later, Flying Swallow won the game. With her amazing agility and reflexes, she had managed to hit several pressure points on Mighty Bull—enough so that he was rendered immobile. Hong had learnt from Meng-Ting early on that by applying pressure to certain areas of the body, blood flow would be interrupted and one might not move for hours.

"Ahem..." The co-manager coughed. "So the winner is—Flying Swallow!"

Amid stunned silence, the young woman stepped gracefully off the stage and strode to the men in charge of the winnings. Apparently, she had staked a sizable amount on herself.

"Damn!" The man near Hong, who had lost half his savings in the previous match, was almost in tears. "All my savings gone and now I owe them as well! Damn!"

Three more competitions. More cheers and hoots from the crowd. Then the betting for the final match—the showdown between the Invincible Yao and a champion boxer from the South was announced.

Hong could feel her hands growing clammy with sweat. She chided herself for being so nervous; she had to stay calm. While she didn't like killing another, even though she had been at the job for a year, the thought of Ah-Ming's depressed little face steeled her nerves.

From the long house that was heavily guarded, the champion boxer from the South marched out. Two armed guards escorted him to the stage.

"Mo! Mo! Mo the King of Fists!" chanted some of his supporters. "Beat down Yao! Break down Yao! Strip him of his title!"

"Yao is invincible!" supporters of Yao shouted back.

"Yao, come out! Show this Southerner a piece of your mind!"

The chanting went on, growing louder and louder. The Southern champion finished warming up and waited on the left side of the stage, his gaze fixed on the other entrance of the long house. Yao should have appeared by now.

"Where is Yao?"

"We want Yao!"

"It's time now!"

Something felt wrong. Hong craned her neck to see where Yao would emerge.

A figure finally appeared.

Manager Liang, the owner of Duel of Death, strode out from the long house. His face was whiter than the finest cooked rice. He leaped on the stage and held up both of his hands, motioning for the crowd to be silent.

"There will be no final match."

Uproar from the crowd.

"What do you mean, no final?"

"I journeyed a whole day to see the match!"

"What happened to Yao? Was he sick?"

Liang held up his hands again. The buzz gradually died away. The manager paused, as though weighing his words.

"The reason for the cancellation is because," he said clearly, "Yao is dead."

14

"Excuse me, but can you tell me if the compound over there belongs to a man called Yao?"

"Yes. It belongs to the Yaos. Mr. Yao lives with his mother."

Fang walked down the street leading to Yao's residence. It was lined with drooping willows and the road itself was smooth and paved with flat stones. He was at first surprised that Yao lived in such a nice neighbourhood—it resembled Chow and Opal's, in fact—but then Yao's status as the star fighter of Duel of Death could certainly allow him to live comfortably. It was just that Fang had not expected the fighter would live in a peaceful, serene environment, as though Yao preferred to be kept out of the hustle and bustle of the world instead of stirring up excitement in the arena.

Fang recalled back at Heavenly Pleasures, when he had met Manager Liang in person for the first time. Fang had been reluctant to see Liang, especially given the premises, but it saved him time enquiring around for Yao's address. He was also surprised at the manager's readiness to tell him, but perhaps the presence of Jade Fairy helped. She had filled Liang's cup with wine and handed it to him with the most graceful curtsy, as though she were serving the emperor.

If only one day Hong would serve him wine like Jade Fairy did... it wouldn't take a dragon throne to make him feel like an emperor.

Fang reached the house. He lifted his hand to knock on the red-lacquered door with a mixture of trepidation and hesitation. It seemed stupid, silly— nay, even ridiculous—to be walking up to Yao's house and asking the fighter if he had murdered Opal. What if Yao's mother was also in the house? What would she say?

No, of course he wouldn't ask Yao outright if he'd killed the girl. He would phrase it differently— something like asking what Yao was doing that day. He first wanted to make sure that Yao wasn't anywhere near Opal's house at that time. A part of him didn't want to accuse Yao, not when he'd discovered that the fighter lived with his mother. Violent as the reports might be, Fang did not feel like incriminating a man who still took care of his old mother.

Fang knocked on the door. To his surprise, it swung open quite easily. Apparently Yao or his mother did not bother to lock it.

"Mr. Yao?" Fang called. "Mrs. Yao?"

Only the sound of a robin chirping answered him. Strange. If no one was home, why was the door unlocked? If Yao was home, then why did no one answer the door?

The door, which was still half-open, revealed a spacious living room that was neatly furnished. The furniture was arranged in an orderly manner and appeared to be spotlessly clean, but a set of muddy footprints on the floor jumped out in stark contrast.

"Yao?" Fang called again. "I'd like to have a few words with you. It won't take long."

Still no answer.

Then he spotted a tiny red stain on the floor. Was it blood?

The uneasiness he was feeling became much stronger, accompanied with a streak of fear. Of course, the blood could be from a heavy bout of training, but still…

Fang entered the living room. There was a door in the far end of the room—it was open. He probably should leave—but curiosity got the better of him. Fang moved to the door and walked past the entrance.

A man lay sprawled on the ground, face to the floor, and a pool of blood near his mouth.

Fang couldn't believe his eyes. Was this—*Yao?*

He crouched, gingerly turned the body over, and promptly received a nasty shock. The man's eyes were wide open, his expression so stiff and frozen that he could only be dead.

Footsteps approached the house.

"Yao! Come out this instant, you have a fight with the Southern champion tonight!"

Another man burst in the room. When he saw Fang kneeling on the floor, cradling the dead body, the newcomer let out a yell.

"Yao! Impossible!"

Fang's fears were confirmed. The Invincible Yao… dead? But there wasn't a knife or sword sticking out from his body. Only the trickle of blood from his mouth. Which meant that someone must have killed the star fighter with bare hands.

"You!" The newcomer stared at him, his eyes cold and hard. "Why did you kill him?"

Hong was dumbstruck. Yao was dead already? Who could have killed him right before his match?

Below the stage, cries of "Unbelievable!" "So sudden!" "Was it a heart attack?" could be heard, mostly in tones of astonishment and irritation. The Southern champion, sitting on the corner of the stage, looked displeased. Obviously, he had been hoping to show off his skills before the audience and destroy Yao's invincibility. Without a worthy opponent, all his plans were now for naught.

Manager Liang held up a hand. It took some time before the crowd had quietened down enough for his voice to be heard.

"As of now, we are still trying to find out the cause of Yao's death. I am sorry to deprive you of a good show, but remember, we still have plenty of excellent fighters at Duel of Death! Tomorrow, we shall arrange for King of Fists to duel with Whirlwind Ko—let me assure you, it shall be a fight not to be missed! The attendance fee will be one string of coppers only—half price off! You may leave now, but don't forget to show up for tomorrow night!"

"Now what's the fun in *that*?" the man whom Hong had talked to earlier said. "Whirlwind Ko may be slippery, but he gives up too easily. If he finds the chance of winning too small, then he'll fake an injury and lose. The show'll be over in less time than an incense stick burning to an end."

Most of the audience seemed to share the same sentiment. Muttering and grumbling, the crowd slowly dispersed.

Hong took one last look at the stage before she left. While Manager Liang was still smiling and entreating the audience to come back, another man with a huge potbelly waddled up to him and whispered something in his ear. Liang's expression changed instantly, but just for a second.

Feeling that Yao's death was no simple matter, Hong slipped away. At least, she would have saved Meng-Ting the expense of some costly drugs.

An hour later, Hong returned to the governor's dwelling. She had rushed to Meng-Ting's place to change her male attire into her usual blue robe.

Meng-Ting wasn't there. Only Ah-Ming was sitting on a tall stool at the counter, crushing some herbs into powder with a ceramic pestle. Probably Meng-Ting was suddenly called away to see a patient.

Since Ah-Ming didn't know about her secret identity, Hong had to sneak in the back door. In a flash she retrieved her maid outfit and wiped off the yellow paint on her face. After double-checking her reflection in the mirror, she hurried back to the governor's.

To her surprise, there was a luxurious sedan chair sitting in front of the main entrance. It had gilded trappings and red satin curtains, clearly belonging to someone of great wealth or status. Four men who looked like official servants loitered nearby, all in navy blue and grey uniforms.

Once in the courtyard, Hong almost bumped into Golden Lotus, who was carrying a large teapot.

"Master Shue is entertaining some guests, I suppose?" Hong asked. "Do you know who the guests are?"

Golden Lotus jumped, nearly sending the teapot crashing to the floor. "Oh, Hong!" she wailed, clearly distressed. "Terrible, terrible news has reached us!"

Hong quickly took the teapot; it was quite heavy for a small woman like Golden Lotus. "What news?"

"They... they say Master Fang has committed murder!"

"*Fang?*" In her surprise, Hong forgot to add the honorific. "What are you talking about? Who did he kill?"

The little maid wiped her face with the back of her sleeve. "I don't know exactly who it is, but the dead person's mother is here, demanding justice. Master Shue is currently with the magistrate in the parlour. Oh dear, I must be going to comfort poor nurse Chang. She was devastated to hear that Young Master Fang had done such a thing. She's been in hysterics and couldn't eat a bite of dinner."

Nurse Chang was the old nurse who cared for Fang and a couple of other sons. It was customary for upper-class families to employ nursemaids to breastfeed babies instead of the biological mother. Fang's mother had passed away early when he was only ten years old. Hong still remembered her—a kind lady who had given her a dainty bronze mirror and even asked if she'd like to become her daughter-in-law when she grew up.

"I must go," Hong said. "Is this tea meant for the guests?" When Golden Lotus nodded, Hong touched her shoulder. "Go to Nurse Chang. I'll take the tea to the parlour."

The parlour was a spacious hall with low mahogany chairs lining both sides of the hall. In the back centre, a larger chair was placed for the master of the house. Here sat Shue Song, his lips tightly pressed. His right hand was gripping his knee, and he looked tired and frustrated. On the left sat his sons and daughter, and Fang looked particularly distressed. Lynn had her hand on his elbow and was glaring at the guests.

On the right side was the magistrate, who was leaning back on his chair with an air of irritation. His expression indicated that he disliked being here and wanted to get the matter over with quickly. Near him was an elderly woman dressed in a rumpled grey robe. Her hair, streaked with white, was messily combed and tendrils were hanging out of her bun. On the left side sat Manager Liang and two other men, presumably from Duel of Death as well. One of them was the co-manager—Hong recognised him from his massive size. The other was a short but muscular young man with an egg-shaped head.

"I demand justice be done!" the old woman shouted. "It was my only son. My only support left in life!"

Fang started to speak, but Shue held up his hand.

"Mrs. Yao, please calm down," Shue said. "I'm terribly sorry to hear of your loss, but there is no proof that Fang committed the crime."

"He was found with my son's body!" shrieked Mrs. Yao, her shrill voice seeming to pierce the roof. "I tell you, I don't care what happens to me. I have no fear as I am going to die soon anyway. But I want to see my son's life avenged!"

Shue looked towards the magistrate. "Who saw my son with the body?"

"Little Tiger did," Manager Liang said, indicating the young man with an egg-shaped head. "I sent him to Yao's and he found your son kneeling over the dead body."

Little Tiger nodded. "Yao was late for his match, so Master Liang had me fetch him."

"Was there a weapon?" Ping suddenly asked.

"Er…" Little Tiger scratched his head.

"Then the death must be of some other cause," Ping said. "It seems impossible that my brother could kill a prized fighter without a weapon. Maybe it was a heart attack? What did the autopsy say?"

"Poison!" screamed the old woman. "My son may be the best fighter in town, but what can he do against lowly tricks?"

"Excuse me," Lynn said sharply. "There is no proof that my brother used poison. Besides, what could he gain from your son's death? Fang never knew him."

"Because he believes Yao killed his friend's wife," Manager Liang said smoothly. "He was avenging his friend."

Shue Song sat up straight. Lynn's jaw fell. Hong clenched her fists and let go. How did they know about Opal's death?

"Are you… referring to Chow's wife?" Shue said slowly.

"My son had never seen that wench since she left him. She was a money-grubber anyway, I didn't think she was a decent sort. You!" Mrs. Yao screeched, stabbing a finger at Fang's direction. "You! Bring back my son's life!"

"Restrain her," Shue said in a low voice. "In case she falls down in a fit."

Two of his men crossed the hall and tried to make Mrs. Yao sit down. She eventually did, but sent Fang a look of pure venom.

Hong bit her lip. She hadn't known that Fang had attempted to confront Yao. But then, who was responsible for Yao's murder? Had the murderer also killed Opal, or were they different people?

Fang walked over to Mrs. Yao, though keeping a reasonable distance away.

"Mrs. Yao, I did not kill your son," Fang said steadily. "He was dead when I found him. I swear it."

Mrs. Yao glared. "Liar! Then why did they find you alone with his body? You thought to get rid of him for your friend, huh? You didn't think you could defeat him so you used poison. I may be old and frail, but I am not afraid of you. I will not rest until my son receives the peace he deserves. Your Honour, I beseech you to take pity on my old age. My son is dead, and I want justice done!"

Magistrate Ho yawned before slowly getting to his feet. "Pardon me, Governor Shue, but I'm afraid that so far all evidence points towards your son. I'll have to bring him in to the tribunal." At his command, two constables strode up and grabbed Fang's arms.

Lynn gasped. "Are you taking him to jail?"

"According to the law, the person accused must be taken in and kept behind bars until the next court hearing." Magistrate Ho said. "Unless you are willing to pay a fine of a thousand taels to guarantee he will show up at court? Otherwise, how am I to answer to the victim's family?" He nodded towards Mrs. Yao, who was still seething with rage.

"I'll pay," Lynn offered. "I can pawn some of the jewellery I've got, and I can…"

"Don't," Ping hissed, pulling on her sleeve. "It's not worth bribing this… this *person*. We'll do our best to gather evidence to exonerate Fang. Wait until the court hearing."

Shue stared at the magistrate unflinchingly. Normally, a magistrate would not dare to arrest a governor's family, not even when the accused was found guilty, but Magistrate Ho rarely concerned himself with other authorities, since he enjoyed favour with the emperor.

"So… I gather there is no fine to be collected?" Magistrate Ho drawled.

Shue did not answer. Instead, he turned to Fang. "Son, stay strong. I believe that you are no murderer. We shall endeavour everything to prove your innocence."

Fang nodded, trying to smile bravely. He had heard of stories of the horrible conditions in jail, but he was certain he could withstand it.

"Take him away," Magistrate Ho ordered.

"I can walk on my own, thank you," Fang said, shaking off the hands of the constables.

Hong wished fervently she could pierce Ho's ears with her trusty poisoned needles. When Fang passed by, she gave him a firm, steadfast look to show that she believed in him. She would do everything she could to find out the real murderer.

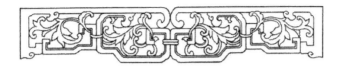

15

The next day, Hong made her way to Mrs. Yao's house, carrying a basket of fruit and flowers. She had made sure to dress up in a plain grey robe, making herself look poor but respectable.

She had to find out who did it. Despite warnings from her *sifu*, Hong knew that she cared for her young master, had done ever since he took her hand and gave her sweets when they were children.

Using the info supplied by one of Old Man Liu's beggar spies, she found the house without much difficulty. Hong knocked on the door. "Mrs. Yao?" she called.

No answer. Hong gave the door a push, and found that it opened easily.

"Mrs. Yao? Hello?"

Hong stepped inside. The interior was cleaner than she expected. A couple of bamboo chairs, a small round wooden table, and a broom stood in a corner. A few leaves lay strewn across the floor, however.

Feeling rather apprehensive, Hong approached another door, which she presumed was the bedroom. She had heard slight movements coming from within.

"Mrs. Yao? This is Hong Sien. I am a maidservant at the governor's, and I have come to say—"

The door swung open. Old Mrs. Yao appeared, her face haggard and her nose red from crying. Without her anger, the wrinkles on her face became more pronounced. She looked older, more tired, more frail. It was hard to imagine that this depressed-looking old woman was the same one whose shrieks could pierce the roof last night.

"Go away."

"I'm sorry, and I commiserate with your loss, but I have to ask you a few questions." Hong held out her basket. "I gather you have no one to give you a hand around. Here, if you can just let me poke around, I can fix you some tea."

"I said go away!" Mrs. Yao glared, though she eyed the basket hungrily. "I don't need your pity. Besides, you're just here to beg me to absolve the murder of your master, right? Well, let me give you some advice. He may be good-looking and well off, but you'll never hold on to him. Men of his station sweet-talk you into their beds and turn their backs as soon as they're tired of you. And what are you—a servant? You'll never be anything more than a toy."

"This has nothing to do with what I came for," Hong said steadily. Briefly, she wondered if Yao's father was "good-looking and well off." Otherwise, why the sudden hatred? "I came to ask you why you are so certain of Master Fang's guilt. According to what I have heard, there are many more who could have done the deed. Master Fang's motive, while understandable, doesn't hold as much weight compared to others."

Mrs. Yao looked away. "He was the one found with my son's body. Anyone at the fighter's ring can tell you that."

"But would not it make more sense if he hadn't stayed?" Hong said. "If you were to poison someone, why would you want to stay and be caught? Master Fang is young and inexperienced, but I doubt he would do something that stupid."

Mrs. Yao sniffed. "How would I know? He killed my son. I demand retribution."

"Mrs. Yao." Hong looked at her intently. "I am very, very sorry for your loss. My parents passed away when I was nine. Were it not for the benevolence of Master Shue, I would have probably ended up in a brothel or begging in the streets. Yet it seems to me that you are more interested in incriminating Master Fang than finding the true murderer. Do not pretend that your son's enemies are limited to Master Fang only."

Mrs. Yao swallowed. Hong held her gaze. Suddenly, the old woman broke down, weeping.

"I know. I knew it from the start. I had begged my son countless times to stop working as a fighter, it's too risky. I pleaded with him to stop drinking so much, it's damaging his health. But he just laughs and tells me that the alcohol only strengthens his fighting ability. He never thinks of the long term, it breaks my heart…"

Hong patted her shoulder, feeling rather sorry for the old woman. It made more sense now. She doubted that Mrs. Yao was really bent on accusing

Fang, unless she had a perfectly good reason for doing so.

"Did anyone put you up to this?" Hong asked quietly.

Mrs. Yao looked away. She twisted her hands and muttered something under her breath.

"Yes?" Hong pressed on.

"It's the magistrate's son. I heard from his servants that Fang had a fight with him, and he's been wanting to get revenge since."

"Ho Jiang-Min?"

Mrs. Yao nodded sullenly. "He told me that he'll give me a tidy sum if I insisted on accusing Fang."

"And you just accepted?" Hong said, disgusted.

"What else was I to do? I'm seventy years old, I only had one son, all the relatives I know are sick or dead. And I did think Fang was most likely. He had the motive and he was present."

Hong put a hand to her forehead. "How much did he give you?"

"A hundred taels of silver. Once Fang is behind the bars, he'll pay me."

Hong pulled out a small pouch from her inner robes. She used to carry some money around for emergencies; sometimes when on her missions, a bribe would be more preferable to shedding blood.

"Here." She held out a silken brooch studded with pearls. "This is worth more than a hundred and fifty taels. Take this now. All I want you to do is to stop accusing Fang and help us find the real murderer."

Mrs. Yao's eyes widened. "How could you— how did you—"

"Take it," Hong said, laying the brooch on her palm. "I owe the governor's family a great deal. I do not want to see Master Fang labelled a murderer. I believe he did not commit this heinous crime."

Mrs. Yao's hand closed over the brooch. "But so far the evidence is strongest against him."

Hong pursed her lips. "That is why I came to ask you. I thought you might shed some light on the issue."

Mrs. Yao thought for a while. "Maybe it was one of the fighters at the ring. There was this man called Whirlwind Ko, he was nicknamed Second Man because he could never beat my son."

Whirlwind Ko? Hong remembered that night at Duel of Death, Ko was to replace Yao in his match with the Southern champion. Could Ko have secretly poisoned Yao, in hopes of claiming the number one spot?

"Thank you very much, Mrs. Yao." Hong rose to leave. "If you know anything, just send a message to the governor's compound. And... again, I'm sorry for your loss."

"You're doing a lot for that young man, aren't you? Did he send you?"

"No, I came of my own accord."

"Well, I'd advise you not to give your all to him. Don't think that he'll be thanking you and offering you a position. Men. They can take things for granted. Go and find an honest, hard-working man. Much more reliable. A young man like him will only break your heart."

"I assure you I have no aspirations," Hong said gravely. "I know my position, and I have no wish to remain in the governor's family permanently. But still,

I'm doing this willingly because I owe the governor a huge debt. Without him, I'd be nothing."

Mrs. Yao pressed a corner of her robe, where she had slipped in the brooch. "I dare say, if they bestowed you with such gifts."

"I'd have done the same even if they didn't give me anything," Hong retorted. A bowl of chicken soup from Fang touched her more deeply than all the brooches and bracelets in the world.

Whirlwind Ko. Now she must try to find out if he was the murderer.

Back at the governor's compound, Hong was immediately summoned to the kitchens. A few servants had come down with the flu and could not be trusted to be near the dishes, and the cook was in a foul mood.

"Don't forget your place, girl," the cook grumbled. "The master may be lenient, but you're doing far less work than other servants. Come and watch over the fire. Don't let the flames die out, or I'll be sending you to clean the privies!"

As a matter of fact, Hong's job did not include kitchen tasks, but since the kitchen was indeed lacking in assistance, she silently went to work. It was also true that she didn't work as much as the other servants, due to her frequent visits to Old Man Liu's place. And she did receive partial treatment from Governor Shue. No wonder that some servants disliked her.

The smoke was unpleasant and she coughed several times, but she did manage to keep the fire burning consistently. Then she was ordered to sweep up food scraps, clean the tables, and carry fresh water from the stone well in the courtyard. Due to her training with Old Man Liu, the menial tasks were not physically draining, but she had to pretend to look weary, such as wiping her forehead from time to time and sitting instead of standing. All the while she worked, she thought about Fang and wondered how to clear his name.

"That should be enough," interjected an elderly servant. "Let the girl off, we're almost done."

The cook sniffed. "All right. But before you go, take this pot of tea to the masters, they've been drinking it by the bucketful."

Hong bowed, keeping her eyes on the ground. "It shall be done."

When she reached the main building, voices floated from within. Hong caught the word "Fang" repeatedly; she paused outside for a moment. Her hearing was acute enough that she could stand at a reasonable distance without seeming like she was eavesdropping.

"So about this Yao…"

"I asked one of the fighters at the ring," Ping was saying. "Bribed them with the best wine of Rose Daughter. They say that it could've been anyone. Yao was universally disliked. One of them said he was going to do him in one day, once he had the chance, and even laments that Fang got to him first."

"The butcher who lives near the Yaos says the same thing," said Gwang, the eldest son. "Yao repeatedly has bought meat but never actually paid up, but since he was the best fighter around, the butcher didn't dare to raise dissent. He says that even without a weapon, Yao had the ability to beat one wielding a knife."

Shue Song furrowed his brow. "If this Yao has been such a criminal, why hasn't he been brought to justice before? Who shielded him?"

"The managers at the fighter's ring, naturally," Ping said. "Yao was bringing them too much business; they didn't want to lose their prized fighter. Most of his victims were poor and insignificant, so they were easily bought off with a couple silvers."

Shue Song crossed his arms. "This ought not happen. I should have a word with the magistrate some time."

His sons didn't say anything, but only looked at each other. Magistrate Ho, though not the kind of ruthless sort who brought commoners grief, was inept and indecisive. If a matter could be solved by the least effort, such as bribes or coercion, he would not take the trouble to do the right thing.

"Well, at least Yao is not a victim to be pitied," Gwang said finally. "What might be the worst for Fang?"

"That crazy old lady demanded his head, but I doubt even the magistrate will concede," Ping said. "Plus, if necessary, we can bribe him too."

"I don't want my son labelled a murderer, especially when the fact remains that he is innocent." Shue Song stood up. "Continue your enquiries. Too bad that I have to leave for the capital tomorrow. An imperial messenger informed me that the emperor has summoned me and the Hwa-Lu District Governor to court."

"Has the emperor given a reason why he wants you and the other governor there?" Gwang asked.

"The Tibetans have been driven back to their regions in the west. Is there the possibility that they will attack again?"

"I do not think so," Shue Song said. "As a matter of fact... I believe this is more a case of domestic conflict. There has been news of the Wei-Bo District governor acquiring more bodyguards than necessary for his compound. He might be trying to assemble his own army."

"Governor Tien?" Ping said. "Why, he already has a reputation for being an outstanding fighter himself. Wasn't there a rumour that he could bend an iron poker with his bare hands?"

"If it's true, then I question the sanity of the person who tries to attack him," Gwang said, grinning.

"That is why the emperor is worried. Who knows if Tien plans to become another An Lushan and raise a rebellion? I suspect His Excellency is trying to make me and the Hwa-Lu governor band together and show our support for the imperial court."

"Not a bad idea, but from what I've heard, the Hwa-Lu governor is useless," Ping said. "I doubt his support will count much against Tien."

"Better use this opportunity to impress upon him the seriousness of Tien as a threat, then," Gwang said. "Father, don't worry about us at home. We'll get Fang out of prison before you're back."

Hong lay on her bed, staring up at the ceiling. She had planned to do her own enquiries the next day, but she couldn't sleep. What Mrs. Yao had told her kept playing through her head. The magistrate's son had

bribed the old woman and told her to accuse Fang...
for what reason?

She sat up. Magistrate Ho had informed them that they would be holding court in three days. She had to search for more information on her own. Old Man Liu's network of beggar spies were useful, but when dealing with people at Duel of Death, she had to act. Time was running out.

Flinging the blanket off the bed, Hong rose and went to her mirror. From the position of the moon in the sky, she judged it to be near midnight. Using what little moonlight was available, she quickly dressed in her black robes for travelling at night. She packed a supply of drugged needles in a pouch, stuck several iron hairpins in her bound hair, and inserted a dagger in her boot.

She listened carefully, ascertained that no human was near, and slipped out of her room.

It was pitch-dark outside and horribly quiet. In her first mission, Hong had wasted a good deal of time overcoming her fear. Old Man Liu had drilled her mercilessly in her ability to hear, ordering her to bear in mind: replace her sight with hearing. When she concentrated on sound, the darkness would not seem so ominous.

Like a sleek Persian cat, Hong headed towards Duel of Death.

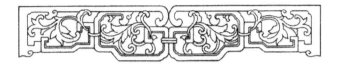

16

Although it was midnight, the buildings at Duel of Death still had lamps burning. Like the brothels and gambling rings, many of the activities continued on well into the night. Sounds of drunken men singing and jesting floated from the area where the duels took place. Hong did not even bother with the front entrance; she darted swiftly to the back and looked for a suitable spot to jump over the wall.

She pressed her ear on the wall and listened for where less human activity was going on. Taking out her hooked sash, Hong threw it into the air. A tug on the sash, and the next second, she leaped on the wall and rested for a brief second, scanning the buildings below. She slipped noiselessly down the wall and retrieved her sash, tucking it securely inside her robes.

Now she had to look for clues. Most of the buildings in the back, which she knew were dwellings of the fighters, were dark. Hong wove her way between the buildings, a couple of drugged needles held between her fingers. All the time she kept her ears trained to pick up every single word and sound.

After a while of vigilant spying, she found what she came for. In the long house, which was situated between the front courtyard and the fighters' residences in the back, she could hear urgent voices that sounded like Manager Liang and his co-manager.

Someone emerged from another building. Hong ducked behind a bush and hoped that she wasn't seen. She couldn't stay in the bush forever, though. It was too far to hear what Liang was talking about.

Hong waited until the man had gone, then moved towards the long house. Using her sash, she landed lightly on the roof. Padding over to the room Liang occupied, she crouched low and pressed her ear to the roof. She couldn't hear them clearly, so she reached for one of her iron hairpins. Prying cautiously, she loosened one of the tiles on the roof. It was risky, but she got what she wanted. She could hear every single word now.

She peered through the crack between the tiles. Manager Liang and his co-manager, a man whom she had heard was nicknamed Potbelly, were sitting by a low table. Empty wine jars scattered around them.

"Damn!" Manager Liang was saying. "This is all your fault. You cooked up this idea. Now I've lost my best fighter."

"Well, who would have known things would get carried too far?" Potbelly drawled. "And wasn't it *you* who was complaining that Yao was getting too full of himself?"

"I just wanted to teach him a lesson," Liang said, his right hand curling into a fist. "Plus, the odds against him winning every fight were getting too easy. A little poison could have tipped the scales in his opponent's favour. I never wanted him dead."

Silence fell. Potbelly reached for another wine jar and poured a cup.

"Do you really think it's that governor's son who did him in?"

Liang gave a contemptuous bark of laughter. "That kid? If he could last five minutes with Yao, I'd hire him on the spot."

"But if the poison had already taken effect…"

"I don't think so. Besides, from the look of that kid, he doesn't know how to spell the word 'murder.'"

"Oh, he's dead meat for sure." Potbelly waved his hand. Two golden rings glittered on his fat fingers. "All evidence points to him. Motivation, location, timing. Heck, if you weren't so sure about the kid, I'd believe it was him! So… did you find out who did it?"

Hong leaned forward. She could hardly breathe.

"Must be one of them," Liang sighed. "I've been telling Yao that he ought to tone down his aggressiveness, but he never took it to heart. Thinks he is head and shoulders above the rest."

"Well, in his defence—he *is* the best fighter we've seen for a decade. So what do you plan to do? Pin the crime on the Fang kid?"

"Of course. That's why I gave him Yao's address—if anything happened, we'd have a ready scapegoat."

Potbelly drummed his fingers on the table. "If it were just a case of drugging, it might be all right. But now there's a dead body involved…"

A shout came from the front courtyard. Hong immediately flattened herself against the roof.

"What?" Liang snapped, going to the window.

"Sir... there's someone on the roof!"

"Huh?"

She couldn't stay any longer. Biting her lip, Hong shimmied across the roof towards the edge, where it curved upwards. Grabbing the curve, she released her hooked sash. It flew and attached on the wall.

"There! There he is!"

A couple of people in the back were shouting and pointing.

She had no time to lose. Hong tugged on the sash, kicked out against the roof tiles, and leaped. Thanks to her sash, she was able to fly all the way from the roof, over the wall, and landed on the ground.

More shouts came behind the wall.

"He's escaped! Get him!"

Hong ran.

Someone was pounding on her door. "Hong! Hong, are you up yet?"

Hong rolled to the inner side of her bed, burrowing her face into the blanket. Sleep, like a sack of sand, weighed heavily on her eyelids.

"Hong! Mistress Lynn is asking for you! Get up this very instant!"

Reluctantly, Hong cracked open an eye. Sunlight was streaming in through the paper lattice on her window. She didn't want to get up—she was still weary from last night—but she had to. She staggered to the door and opened it.

"What are you doing?" Golden Lotus said in an annoyed voice. "Honestly, you shouldn't be sleeping in on a day like this! Get dressed as soon as you can. We're to go to Mrs. Guo's today."

"Wh… who?"

Golden Lotus brushed past her, soaked a handkerchief in the water basin, and threw it on her face. "Wake up!"

A few minutes later, Hong was dressed and ready to go. As long as she wasn't putting on a disguise, she barely needed any time for her simple robe and hairstyle. When she was done, Golden Lotus grabbed her arm and steered her towards Lynn's residence.

"Take your lute," Golden Lotus said. "Mistress Lynn said that we might need it."

Hong didn't understand. "Why are we going to Mrs. Guo's? Do you mean the magistrate's daughter who has recently married Merchant Guo's eldest son?"

"Of course. Things have gone worse for Master Fang! Now there are rumours going around that he actually *coveted* Opal, and that he killed Yao to avenge her."

Hong stopped. "Ridiculous." First, Fang had never showed any interest towards Opal. Second, even if he had, wouldn't it have made more sense to get rid of her husband, rather than a former lover?

"Ain't it so? Mistress was furious when the news reached us. She's going to see if she can persuade Mrs. Guo to talk to her father. Oh, and since Mrs. Guo seemed to like your music, Mistress Lynn said that you ought to go as well."

Hong would have preferred to pay Duel of Death another visit, to find out who Manager Liang was referring to, but after her spying last night, perhaps it'd be a better idea to wait for a while. The security at Duel of Death would most likely be tightened.

Lynn was waiting for them impatiently.

"There you are," she said briskly. "Come on, we should be going. Hong, have you brought your lute?"

"Yes."

"Good. Mrs. Guo wrote me a while ago that she wanted to hear the song you performed at Father's banquet, but she couldn't because she just got married and was supposed to stay home. If you keep her in a good mood, then it'll be easier to speak up for Fang."

"As you say, Mistress."

The Guo residence was located in the wealthiest part of town, among several other huge compounds. Few people loitered in the streets; it differed much from the noisy chatter and jostling crowds in the market area. When Hong walked slowly on the well-paved stone road, she reflected that although it was also peaceful, the affluent area wasn't the same as her *sifu's* place. Old Man Liu's compound was remote and quiet, yet she could feel a sense of peace and calm when playing her flute under one of the willow trees. Here, with every step of her leather shoes echoing on stone, she felt like a thief intruding on someone's property.

Presently, Lynn's sedan chair stopped in front of a large red door, which had a pair of stone lions sitting in front of it. Four expressionless guards stood outside, each carrying long staffs and swords. One of them had a scar running down from his right ear to his left jowl.

"They certainly keep their place well guarded," Golden Lotus whispered. "Not even our home can compare to this."

Hong scanned the guards with a brief yet piercing gaze. From their postures and the way they moved, she could tell they were well trained—possibly first-class fighters, only secondary to the likes of Invincible Yao. The Guos must be immensely wealthy to employ such guards—four indeed! Normally one or two should be sufficient.

Lynn got out of the sedan.

"I am Lady Lynn, Governor Shue's daughter," she said in a loud, clear voice. "Please inform Wen-Jun—I mean Mrs. Guo—that her friend has come to visit."

Lynn was dressed in bright colours of yellow and pink. An expensive-looking jade pendant dangled from her throat, and her golden bangles jangled when she raised her hand.

One of the guards went inside, another politely asked Lynn to wait, while the two others surveyed Hong and the other maidservants. Unsurprisingly, their eyes lingered on Golden Lotus longer. Golden Lotus was easily the prettiest girl in their group, with shiny hair the colour of black silk, and big sparkling eyes framed by long curved lashes. Her skin was pink and white, like plum blossoms.

"The young mistress bids them enter." The guard who had disappeared inside had returned, accompanied by the steward of the house, who bowed towards Lynn.

"Please follow me, madam."

The Guo residence was magnificent enough to justify the number of guards. Pillars of marble, with gilded dragons wound over them; winding corridors with carved patterns in the railings and ceilings; in the garden, there was an artificial lake big enough for a few boats. A glittering pavilion built from glazed tiles stood at the edge of the lake, with semi-transparent curtains made of the finest gossamer-like silk.

"Lynn?" A young woman, exceedingly beautiful, came towards them. She was dressed in a peach-coloured brocaded robe which gleamed from the intricate golden threads woven into it. Dewdrop-shaped pearl earrings dangled from her ears, and she wore a long necklace of exquisite beads. Hong remembered Mrs. Guo—she looked exactly the same as before, lovely enough to break a million hearts. The only difference was that she now wore her hair completely pinned up in a tight bun, the sign of a married woman.

Hong also recognised Little Jade, one of Mrs. Guo's personal handmaids, who was hovering near her mistress as though she'd fall and twist her ankle. Were it not for her delicate constitution, Magistrate Ho would certainly have tried to send his second daughter into the emperor's harem as well.

"I am so glad to see you." Mrs. Guo enveloped her friend in a hug and let go. "Bring us the tea wrapped with tangerine peel that Father bought two days ago," she told Little Jade. "And some of the cakes we had yesterday. Oh, and the exotic litchi fruit they keep sending from the south. We must have a feast."

When the food was brought, served in silver plates gilded with gold, Lynn couldn't help exclaiming,

"Such luxury! So nice it is to marry into wealth! Perhaps arranged marriages are not as frightening as I've heard."

"There are downsides." Mrs. Guo wrinkled her small, pert nose. "I have to get up extremely early every day and bring tea for my in-laws. My mother-in-law is especially particular with the steeping of tea, so I don't even ask the servants to do it. I am now a master of tea-brewing—and to think I had never stoked a fire before. Incredible, isn't it?"

"I suppose it's difficult. The smell from the pot reminds me of the herbal medicines I had to take when I had a cold." Lynn shuddered. "I would prefer to have cold pressed orange juice or honey cinnamon water."

"And I don't get to see my husband often. He just left for the capital this morning. We are just married for ten days. But I hope it was enough." Mrs. Guo blushed. "I want to surprise him with a round belly when he comes back."

Lynn also flushed; as outspoken she was, she was still a maiden. Golden Lotus hid part of her face with a hand.

"Well, I am glad that your marriage has turned out well," Lynn said sincerely, laying a hand on her friend's arm. "Did your parents ask of your opinion before you were married?"

Mrs. Guo's hand quivered; a drop of tea trickled down her cup, and she hastily dabbed it away with her handkerchief. "No… not really. It wasn't like I had a choice, I had to marry someone of equal station."

Lynn blew a strand of her hair out of her eyes. "Father promised me that I can choose for myself, though I doubt he'd give his consent if I announced I plan to marry the gardener."

"You shouldn't have to worry," Mrs. Guo smiled encouragingly. "You are the governor's daughter. No one will dare to harm you."

Lynn took a bite of the cake. It almost seemed sacrilege to destroy the shape of the cake; it was moulded into the petals of a plum blossom, so small and delicate.

"Wen-Jun," she began. "There is something else I came for. Can you help me?"

Instantly, a guarded expression fell over Mrs. Guo's perfect features, like a cloud blotting over the sun.

"Let me guess… it's your brother, isn't it?"

"Have you heard the rumours? They… they say Fang was involved with your former maid, Opal, and when he found her dead, he assumed Yao had killed her. Therefore, he found a chance to poison Yao. Don't you find this just plain ridiculous?"

Mrs. Guo laid down her cup. "I might be cooped up in this maze of a compound every day, but it doesn't mean I've lost my ears. Little Jade has told me a lot. She told me that Fang had asked her about Opal's death."

"But *you* know my brother couldn't possibly be in love with Opal!" Lynn cried. "Indeed, what a ludicrous idea! He has been—well, you know he isn't the kind of person to go around poisoning others!"

Mrs. Guo sighed, looking down at her lap. "First Opal, then Yao, and now Fang is arrested. How tragic things have become."

Lynn reached forward and took both of her hands, looking at her beseechingly. "Wen-Jun, I beg you to talk to your father. Tell him that Fang didn't do it. Tell him Fang didn't murder Yao."

"I... not that I don't want to, but you might be overestimating the influence I have over Father. It's unlikely he will listen to me. Besides, I cannot prove that Fang is innocent. From what I've heard, he was the person who had seen Yao just before his death."

"But you can try, won't you?" Lynn said desperately. "You know Opal and Yao, and you know Fang. What better judge of their characters than you? If you can persuade the magistrate that Fang was never involved with Opal, then it would make his motive for murdering Yao look weaker. Please, Wen-Jun. It's not just for Fang, it's for your maid as well. Surely you don't want Opal's reputation being slandered after her death?"

Golden Lotus and Hong bowed low, and Little Jade joined in. "Oh please, Mistress! We don't want to see Master Fang in prison. He was ever so nice when he visited us."

Mrs. Guo finally nodded. "All right. But don't expect too much. Father's awfully traditional. He probably wouldn't like me interfering with his job."

"There's not much time until the hearing, so can you come out tomorrow?" Lynn said. "It's the Cold Food Festival. I say it's a lot more likely that the magistrate will be in a good mood, playing polo and drinking wine with his colleagues!"

Mrs. Guo hesitated. "My in-laws may not like my going out. Since I may be carrying the Guo family's first son, they have been very strict with my daily activities. They'd rather that I not leave the compound."

"But if you can't leave, how are you going to talk to your father?" Lynn said. "Please, Wen-Jun."

They spent some time deciding on what strategy to approach the magistrate with, until a servant announced the return of the elder Mrs. Guo. It would not do if her daughter-in-law was found spending idle hours with her maiden friends. According to tradition, she should be sitting in her room and doing embroidery work. Not wanting to evoke the bad graces of the elder Mrs. Guo, Lynn felt that she ought to go.

"See you tomorrow, then," Lynn said. "Wen-Jun, I know it's difficult for you to leave the house, but if anything can help Fang…"

Mrs. Guo nodded. "I understand. I will be there."

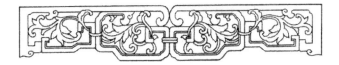

17

When they left the Guo residence, Golden Lotus proposed a detour to the market.

"I'm going to buy some nice food at the market," she announced. "Think of Young Master Fang starving in prison! He needs to have nutritious food delivered to him."

"Well, according to the law, the family is responsible for the prisoner's meals anyway, unless they live cities away," Silver Peony said. "Let us buy all the things that Master Fang likes. If we can't save him now, at least we must save his stomach."

"Agreed!" Golden Lotus said, clapping her hands. "We'll do our best on the festival and make the magistrate see sense."

"He must," Lynn said fervently. "Remember how he looked when he came to our home? How I want to slap his face! He didn't even bother to ask Fang the details—he only wanted a culprit so he wouldn't be wasting time looking for the real murderer."

"Poor Master Fang," Silver Peony sighed. "It's just too bad that he happened to be at the wrong place at the wrong time. Let's make the biggest batch of food we can and bring it to him."

While the three girls discussed animatedly what food they should prepare for Fang, Hong remained silent. She was still pondering who the murderer could be. According to her brief spying in Duel of Death, it must be some insider. "Must be one of them," Manager Liang had said. Them? Who could it be?

She was rather listless when picking through the vegetables and fruit. Hong had never been a good cook; she was more adept at boring, menial tasks like stoking the fire and washing the dishes. Plus, many years of visiting Old Man Liu had accustomed her taste buds to bland, simple food that often consisted of white rice and boiled greens only. Old Man Liu might have lived at court in his youth, but now in his old age, he lived like a monk.

"Master Ping!" Silver Peony suddenly said. "And isn't that Shu-Mo?"

Hong raised her head. Indeed, Ping and Shu-Mo were walking down the street, just several paces away.

"Brother!" Lynn hurried over to them. "How did it go with you? Have you found out anything that might help Fang?"

"Not bad," Ping said with a grin. "I bribed some fighters at Duel of Death, along with Rose Daughter's best wine, and they blabbed. Seems that there's a fighter called Whirlwind Ko—"

"Whirlwind Ko?" Hong said without thinking. So that must be the person Manager Liang had been referring to.

Ping cast her a wary look, but Lynn was urging him to continue.

"Ko cooked up a lowly scheme with the co-manager Potbelly. Whirlwind Ko had wanted to see Yao go down in a fight and Potbelly suggested that they purchase some drugs and poison Yao's wine. Yao was a great drinker, you see."

"So they are the ones who poisoned Yao!" Lynn said excitedly.

"I was suspicious when that man called Little Tiger burst in soon after Fang found Yao dead," Ping said grimly. "Seems to me that they had planned it well in advance—Manager Liang definitely knew about the poisoning as well. Yao was bringing in business, but not as profitable as before. He was too powerful—there isn't much to be had for laying the odds against him. If Manager Liang had told a select few to bet against Yao—well, that's a pile of money to be made."

"Those scumbags. Too bad that Fang chose the same day to visit Yao! If only it had been a day earlier!"

"Still, there are a couple of things I'm not sure of," Ping said, frowning. "If the plan was to drug Yao only, why did Yao end up dead? Seems more reasonable to have him lose a battle on stage. With his death, the fight arena can't make any more profits."

"Maybe he was allergic to the drug or he had a latent disease?" Lynn said. "Well, this certainly looks better for brother Fang. Imagine Duel of Death poisoning their own fighter!"

"And where have you been?" Ping said.

"I was at Wen-Jun's—though she should be called Mrs. Guo now. I tried persuading her to talk to her father. She was reluctant in the beginning, but she's finally agreed to plead for Fang. She'll be attending the Cold Food Festival tomorrow, where the magistrate will definitely be present. Hopefully the magistrate will listen—even if Wen-Jun isn't his favourite daughter, she still has made a brilliant match."

"Good," Ping said. "Though by the sound of it, you seem awfully pleased that Miss Ho—I mean, Mrs. Guo—will be at the festival. Isn't this an annual event that most girls wouldn't miss?"

"It's different for her, now that she has married," Lynn retorted. "Especially since she is carryi—well, let's say her in-laws are pretty strict." She sighed. "Wen-Jun wasn't audacious when she was a maiden, but still, I'm surprised that she became even more timid—like a mouse. I feel if I touch her, she's going to shatter into pieces."

"Well, make sure you keep an eye on her," Ping said. "Don't want to risk the wrath of either the Guos or the magistrate."

Meanwhile, Shu-Mo was trying to convince Golden Lotus and Silver Peony not to visit Fang.

"It's a terribly filthy place," he said. "You don't want to be there, trust me. I had a friend who was in there for three days only—got caught for petty stealing—and he wasn't the same person when he emerged!"

"All the more reason we should show Master Fang our support," Golden Lotus said indignantly.

"I don't think they'd treat Master Fang *that* badly," Silver Peony mused. "As a governor's son, he would deserve a private cell at least."

"I still say you girls are being too naive..." Shu-Mo grumbled.

"Mr. Shu-Mo?" a voice came from behind him. "No letters to write today?"

It was Calligrapher Pai, who was smiling broadly, an ink brush in hand.

"No, not today," Shu-Mo hissed, trying to convey silently that he did not want to be talked to.

But Golden Lotus and Silver Peony were already watching him suspiciously.

"Why, Shu-Mo, I didn't know you couldn't write."

"What made you want to hire a professional calligrapher, huh?"

As Shu-Mo tried to fend off the maids' questioning, Hong allowed herself a small smile. Now that she knew the names of the people behind the murder, and that Mrs. Guo had promised to speak for Fang, things were definitely looking up.

But only temporarily.

Hong sat on the grass, idly picking at a daisy. A light breeze blew by and ruffled her hair. Spring had arrived.

The city park was full of people coming out to enjoy the Cold Food Festival. Some brought colourful kites, others had bamboo spinning toys. A group of children were playing with a shuttlecock made of feathers—whoever failed to catch the feathered toy with her knee or foot would be deemed the loser. Several girls were doing a popular "step-dance" along the river bank, a routine consisting of singing and dancing.

Magistrate Ho, attired in an expensive-looking brocaded robe, was just stepping off his velvet sedan. Two of his concubines, also dressed in costly dresses and decked out in pearls and jade, hung on his arms. The magistrate's procession settled in a large pavilion near the lake. Servants carrying food baskets came up and soon a feast was laid out in the pavilion.

Normally, an outing in the park was a joyous event, especially for the maids at Governor Shue's. But today they were tense and even nervous. Although Ping had uncovered the dirt on Duel of Death, a lot still depended on the magistrate's attitude. For most districts, the local officer was like an emperor, and his word was law.

"All right," Lynn was saying. "We shall wait until the magistrate is drunk. When his senses are addled, Wen-Jun can go talk to him. By the way, has anyone seen Wen-Jun around? She should have arrived long ago."

The maids all craned their necks and looked around, but it was no easy task. There were so many people running around and playing in the park. Furthermore, plenty of trees and bushes and hedges in the park obstructed their view.

"I hope she's all right," Lynn said worriedly. "Do you think her pregnancy might have anything to do with it? Maybe her mother-in-law discovered she was going to the park and forbade her to come?"

"Could be," Silver Peony said. "I mean, look at all these people in the park. If I were her mother-in-law, I'd be a bit worried too."

"But she made a promise," Lynn said. "If she couldn't come, she would have at least sent Little Jade, or some other maid, to tell us that she couldn't make it."

Suddenly, a shout came from Golden Lotus.

"Something weird is happening on the lake!"

At her announcement, Lynn and Silver Peony sprang up.

"What happened?"

Hong squinted. A young woman had stepped in one of the boats by the lake and nearly lost her balance.

"That looks like the magistrate's new concubine," Lynn said. Her tone was of amusement, not worry.

"I bet she's never been on a boat before," Golden Lotus said contemptuously.

"Wait," Silver Peony said. "It doesn't seem to be just clumsiness. Look, her shoes are all wet."

The young woman had hopped back to the river bank, and a good two inches of her robes were soaked. She was gesturing to the boat and shouting furiously.

Many people had gathered around the river bank.

"There's a hole in the boat!" the woman shouted. "I nearly fell into the river and drowned! I want my money back!"

The boatman apologised quickly. "I am so sorry, madam. I had no idea of what happened to the boat. How about changing to another one?" He mentioned nothing of refunding her, however.

"Hey!" one of the people waiting to get on the boat shouted. "If you don't want to get on the boat, there're still plenty of us waiting!"

The woman looked around and sullenly decided to choose another boat that looked newer.

"Pull that one over here," she instructed. She squeezed water from her skirts and stepped into the new boat.

Splash! Another scream. This time the boat actually overturned, taking the unfortunate woman down with her.

"Aaaaaaah!"

"Quick, jump in! Get her out of the river!"

"The water's shallow enough by the bank. Let her come up herself."

The boatman quickly hauled the rest of the boats to the bank. He looked at each of them, then used his oar to prod the floor of one boat. The oar pierced the boat as easily as though it were made of saw dust.

"What's wrong with these boats?" Golden Lotus said. "Are they *all* sabotaged?"

"Look at the magistrate," Silver Peony said. "He seems mighty displeased."

Magistrate Ho was far away and had his back to them, but it was still easy to see him waving at the boatman, who kept bowing and shaking his head.

"Hong, do you mind staying here and waiting for Wen-Jun? Give a shout if you see her, would you?"

"Certainly, Mistress."

Lynn and the other maids hurried towards the boats. A sense of foreboding came over Hong. She already had doubts about Magistrate Ho listening to his daughter. Now with Mrs. Guo absent and the magistrate in a bad mood, it looked like their mission would be futile.

A movement behind a tree caused her to turn around.

"… easy there, oh, won't you sit down?"

Mrs. Guo had finally appeared, escorted by Little Jade. Her face was as grey as a cloudy sky and she was vomiting into a lacquered bowl.

Alarmed, Hong rushed over to her.

"Milady! Should I call for a physician? Or your midwife?" she added, unsure which was more appropriate.

Mrs. Guo wiped her mouth and chin with an expensive silk handkerchief. Hong winced; surely a plain cotton one would do. That silk handkerchief could feed a poor family of four for a week.

"No… I…" Mrs. Guo struggled to speak. "I shall be fine. I thought that I had got over the morning sickness, but it's still with me. No, don't call for anyone. I'll be returning home soon. We keep a physician at home."

Little Jade put a hand on her mistress's back.

"Sorry, but you see how my mistress's condition is. She shouldn't be going to her father now—actually, she shouldn't even be out! Please convey to the governor's daughter that we cannot help now."

"All right," Hong said. Clearly, today was a total failure. "Shall I call a sedan for Mistress Guo?"

By this time, the crowd at the river bank had dispersed. Another boatman was employed to bring a new fleet of boats. Lynn, Golden Lotus, and Silver Peony returned, wearing expressions of annoyance.

"Maybe the river spirit was making mischief overnight..." Silver Peony was saying.

"There's no such thing as a river god," Lynn chided her. "Wen-Jun! You've come! What happened to you?"

Mrs. Guo had stopped throwing up, but her face was still pale. Her hand shook as she held her handkerchief. Hong explained quickly.

"Oh that's too bad," Lynn said. "You have to go home right away! Is your sedan waiting at the edge of the park? Here, let me walk with you."

"So... sorry," Mrs. Guo whispered. "Another time... maybe."

"It's all right, and besides, your father is simply furious now. Someone had sabotaged the boats on the river. What a nasty prank, especially since it's the Cold Food Festival!"

If she weren't still keeping her identity a secret, Hong could have offered to carry Mrs. Guo on her back. The young woman indeed looked quite ill. Unlike Lynn, who was used to playing sports with her brothers and servant maids since she was a child, Mrs. Guo appeared to have been brought up as though she were a glass doll. With her pregnancy, her condition seemed even worse.

They hadn't accomplished what they came for. And the court hearing was tomorrow.

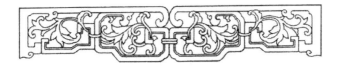

18

Hong paced in her room restlessly. She told herself to calm down. The worst would not happen. Fang was the governor's son; the magistrate would not dare to sentence him to the executioner's axe. Besides, she had extracted from Mrs. Yao that the magistrate's son had offered a bribe. The old woman would not press charges.

Still, it didn't alter the fact that things looked bad for Fang. If any public flogging or scourging left permanent scars on him, he'd be humiliated for life. Besides... who knew what actual punishment the magistrate might give? There were torture mechanisms that were said to be worse than death.

Hong had originally wanted to do some more investigating, to find out who exactly was planning to poison Yao, but a second visit to Duel of Death the night before had been unsuccessful. Manager Liang had acquired several huge black wolfhounds; she had been shocked when she perched on the wall and found several pairs of green eyes glowing in the dark. One started to bark; she had to slip away and run as fast as she could. She could have silenced them with a drugged needle, but the people at the fight arena were already alerted. She was there to spy, not pick a fight.

She had questioned Mrs. Yao and paid two visits to Duel of Death. So far, all she knew was that the real murderer was someone else in the fight arena, but she didn't have enough time to find out.

"Hong!" Golden Lotus rapped on her door. "Hong, are you coming?"

"Of course!" Hong called. Hastily, she double-checked her reflection in the mirror, making sure her face powder was applied thickly enough to conceal the dark circles under her eyes. She had barely slept for more than two hours the night before.

Golden Lotus's eyes were red from crying. "Do you think Young Master will be all right? Do you think he'll be tortured?"

"Nonsense," Hong said, patting her arm. "Young Master is the governor's son. He *will* be treated with respect. Even if Magistrate Ho is the emperor's father-in-law, he will not risk the good will of Master Shue."

"But... but if they can't find the murderer, and Young Master is the most obvious suspect..."

"The gods above are not blind," Hong said steadily. "They will not let an innocent be subjected to unjust punishment."

Her words didn't sound convincing, though, however much she wanted to believe them. Her own father had been innocent, but a few words from a corrupted official had stripped him of everything. And her father had been a well-respected man of considerable wealth. If a rich man could be brought to ruin easily, then there must be countless other poor innocents who had insufficient means to carry them through trials. Hong had heard many stories of poor, ordinary folk who were wrongly accused, injured, or punished.

Hong put her hands together and prayed that the worst would not happen.

Hong had never been to the magistrate's court hall before, but she disliked it on first sight. It was impressively large, yes, but also drab, grey, and austere. On the very end rose a dais, on which was the magistrate's desk. A placard with the phrase "Just and Judicious as the Blue Sky" written in huge characters was hung over the desk. The sergeants and lieutenants stood in two rows on either side, carrying iron poles, which would draw blood if used on criminals. However, iron poles weren't the only instruments available. To the right, a torture mechanism consisting of sharp bamboo sticks hung on the wall. Hong had heard stories that in order to torture a criminal into confession, the sticks would be driven into the criminal's nails. If Magistrate Ho dared to try that on Fang... to hell with reservations of being discovered. She had her glass needles concealed in her sleeves.

Golden Lotus stood near her, trembling. The girl was usually bright and vivacious, but confronted with the court, she was reduced to a timid thing. Lynn, however, had her fists clenched and her expression determined. Fang's two elder brothers, Gwang and Ping, were looking pale and grim. Hong gathered that they had not found any new clue that would exonerate Fang. Chow, dressed in dark robes with a pinned white flower for mourning, was ashen white and looked on the verge of collapsing.

On the other side of court stood Manager Liang and Potbelly. Liang darted a look at them and smirked. No doubt he was confident that Fang would be punished.

In the end of the court, behind a row of constables, were dozens of citizens curious to hear about the trial.

"His Honour has come!" a lieutenant called. Immediately, the sergeants began to rattle the iron poles, thumping them on the ground. The rattling was supposed to create an intimidating effect on the accused.

Magistrate Ho was dressed in full ceremonial robes, a black silk cap perched on his head. He ambled to his seat and sat down. He rapped the gavel on the table, and the thumping ceased.

"Let the first session of this tribunal be opened," he said. "Bring the accused forward."

Between two constables, Fang slowly emerged from a side entrance and stood before the magistrate, his back straight and his head held high. Chains jingled from his wrists, his face was dirty, and the stubble of a beard was visible. He looked thinner than usual—no trace of the confidence he usually carried—but he did not look frightened.

"Shue Fang, third son of Governor Shue Song. You have been accused of the murder of Yao Chian, also nicknamed Yao the Invincible, the star wrestler at Duel of Death. Do you admit to this crime?"

"I do not," Fang replied calmly. "I was merely at the wrong place at the wrong time, Your Honour."

"Oh?" Magistrate Ho leaned forward. "Bad timing, you say? Do you know the deceased?"

"Not personally."

"Then explain why you were found in the same room with the deceased."

"I…" Fang paused, apparently considering how to phrase his speech. "I only wanted to question Yao. He was suspected to be involved with my friend's wife—who died suddenly a while ago. So I asked Manager Liang for his address. When I arrived, I found him dead already. He was lying on the floor. I was going to call for help, but a man from Duel of Death burst in and called me a murderer."

"Interesting story," Ho said. "But anyone can claim what you just said. How are we to believe you did not intend to avenge on your friend's behalf? Or how can we be sure you are not avenging the woman you love?"

Snickers came from some of the onlookers.

Fang flushed. "Opal was my friend's wife! I have nothing, absolutely nothing to do with her."

"Are you sure? There have been witnesses who saw you two together in an alley. Alone."

This time, it was not the magistrate speaking. A young man dressed in expensive robes had appeared, and he was standing near Ho. It was Ho Jiang-Min, the magistrate's son. Fang's eyes narrowed at sight of him.

"That was because you were molesting her! Had I not passed by, she would have cuckolded her husband!"

Another murmur ran through the crowd.

"What nonsense!" Jiang-Min snapped. "Why'd I pick on a married woman when I have so many others at home?"

"Your Honour," Gwang spoke up. "Invincible Yao is known to be the star fighter of Duel of Death. My brother is competent, but he wouldn't go looking for trouble. He only wished to learn the truth."

"Furthermore," Ping added, "we have evidence that it is Duel of Death that decided to poison Yao, so that they could reap benefits at the next competition."

An uproar was raised. People were whispering and pointing at Manager Liang, whose expression changed for a second, but soon he was back to normal, smiling as though nothing had happened.

"Evidence?" Magistrate Ho said. "Duel of Death has been around for years, young man. What evidence can you provide?"

"The owner of Luo's Winehouse has told us that the co-manager of Duel of Death has talked to him." Ping raised a hand and pointed to Potbelly. "Mr. Luo said that he was advised to bet on the Southern champion instead of Invincible Yao. Were Yao truly to lose, Mr. Luo was to split his winnings half and half."

"Ridiculous," Potbelly said, smiling. "I never said such a thing to Mr. Luo. Why would I bet against my own fighter?"

"Call for Mr. Luo," Gwang said. "Then we can ascertain if Duel of Death is staging their own cheating or not."

"But Yao is dead!" Manager Liang said loudly. "Are you implying that we had planned to kill our own champion? How absurd! Why would we choose to do something destructive when Yao has been bringing us so much business? I'd say half, nay, most of the audience at Duel of Death are there to see him fight!"

His voice echoed off the walls. Many of the citizens outside began to nod and whisper that Manager Liang had a point.

"Your Honour," Potbelly said. "When one of our men, Little Tiger, caught Mr. Fang leaning over Yao's body, he also discovered a wine jar on the table. The coroner testified that the wine contained a lethal dose that overpowered Yao. Even a helpless child can kill Yao with this poison." He pointed a fat finger at Fang. "Is this not enough to explain that Mr. Fang is fully capable of overpowering our prized fighter? It doesn't matter that Yao is more powerful—"

"Your Honour!" Gwang raised his voice and took a step forward. "They are trying to evade the issue that they had intended to poison Yao! Please, if you can just let us call for Mr. Luo—"

"Silence!" Magistrate Ho rapped the gavel on the table. "Mr. Gwang, were it not for the fact you are Governor Shue's son, I would have you slapped on the mouth for interrupting the session. You have heard Manager Liang speak, it's absurd they should want to kill their own fighter."

"Due to the strange nature in which Yao died, we searched the house more thoroughly. On the floor, we found this." Manager Liang extracted a piece of crumpled paper from his breast pocket. He held it up in plain view.

Hong's heart beat wildly. On the paper was the stamped imprint of—

"This comes from the store of Liu Meng-Ting. There is still a bit of poisonous powder on it. The coroner has testified that the powder is the same that poisoned Yao."

"Indeed?" Magistrate Ho leaned his elbows on the table. "So what you mean is that Mr. Liu worked in cahoots with Mr. Fang? That they plotted together to do away with Mr. Yao?"

"I do not dare to presume that was the truth, Your Honour," Liang replied, though his expression was smug. "But it is known that the physician has remained on intimate terms with the governor's people. I've heard that one of the maids has frequented Mr. Liu's apothecary."

Hong bit her lip. Obviously he was referring to her.

"Where is Liu Meng-Ting?" Magistrate Ho said.

Liang smirked. "If Your Honour permits, my men have the apothecary in their hands right now. Outside."

"Then what are you waiting for? Bring them in!"

Hong clenched her fists—unseen, for her hands were concealed under her long sleeves. It was obvious that Magistrate Ho was taking sides—he refused to summon Mr. Luo, but did not hesitate to call for Meng-Ting.

A couple of fighters from Duel of Death strode in the tribunal. One had a large hand clamped on the shoulder of a young man.

Meng-Ting. His cap was askew and his knees were shaking.

"Kneel down!"

Meng-Ting hesitated before slowly lowering himself on the floor.

"So." Magistrate Ho regarded the physician with a disapproving eye. "You are Liu Meng-Ting? You keep a store full of drugs in the western district?"

"I do."

"Well, then. Mr. Liu, do you recognise this?" Magistrate Ho indicated the paper on Liang's hand.

Meng-Ting's eyes widened. "It… it is from my store, Your Honour," he stammered.

"What nerve you have! Your poison has been found in the house of Yao Chian, who died four days ago. Can you give an explanation for this?"

Meng-Ting paused, staring at Manager Liang. "I… received an order from Duel of Death to supply a drug that will dull one's senses. I prepared the drug. That is the only way I can conceive that my wrapper has been found there."

"A drug that will dull the senses?" Magistrate Ho sneered. "Would this drug be powerful enough to kill a fighter whose strength has been unequalled? Would it not be more reasonable to say that Mr. Fang has ordered the poison from you, so he can get rid of Mr. Yao easily?"

"But Your Honour… anyone could have bought a drug from me. My wrappers are easy to procure."

Ho thudded the gavel on the table. "Are you questioning my authority, young man?"

"Mr. Liu," Manager Liang said smoothly. "The coroner said that the poison used was called Three-Steps-to-Hell. It is a rare poison, one that is so strong that after taking it, a person will be dead after he takes three steps. Are you saying that this poison is easy to

165

procure as well? Look." He showed the white powder on the paper. "Care to tell us if this is the poison from your store?"

Meng-Ting trembled. But under the stern gaze from the magistrate, he moved forward and sniffed. His face fell.

"Impossible," he whispered.

"Ha! So you admit that the poison came from you! Enough—this hearing has dragged far too long. Three days later, I shall open the session again. If no further evidence is offered by that time, then the verdict for both criminals shall be issued." Ho rapped his gavel. "Mr. Liu Meng-Ting has been found guilty of providing the means of death. Arrest him!"

"Wait," Hong blurted. Without thinking, she came forward.

"Who are you?" Magistrate Ho stared at her, his expression hostile.

"I'm a servant at Governor Shue's," Hong replied, her heart beating wildly. "I am friends with Liu Meng-Ting, and I know him. I beseech you, Your Honour, not to send him to jail."

"Your Honour." Manager Liang spoke up. "I believe that this is the maid whom I referred to earlier. The one who might have passed the drugs to Fang."

"Hmph!" Magistrate Ho leaned back and glared at her. "Do you want me to find you guilty as well? Guards, take both of them away!"

"But…"

"If you interfere with court procedure, I'll have you taken away as well!"

Hong clenched her fists and willed herself to be still. It was very hard not to reach for a glass needle and send it straight at the magistrate's stupid forehead.

But she couldn't. She had to stay behind and do her best to find out the real murderer. If she was locked away behind bars, she couldn't do anything.

19

Hong felt bad after the additional arrest of Meng-Ting. She had thought things would work out, that Manager Liang, Potbelly, and Whirlwind Ko would be found guilty, that Fang would be released. Now she had to seek a way to free them both. *If* there was a way. Under corrupt officials like Magistrate Ho, a fair hearing was only available to those willing to empty their pockets for those in power.

That night, after the hearing, she went straight to her room and locked the door. Golden Lotus and the others were too distressed about Young Master Fang to care about her, and besides, Hong's expression had clearly conveyed that she wished to be left alone.

Tossing and turning on the bed, Hong contemplated what she ought to do. What she really would like to do was to pay the magistrate a visit when he was in bed, press a dagger against his throat, and make him free Fang and Meng-Ting. But, tempting as the thought was, it wouldn't solve the problem completely. She still needed to bring the real murderers, the conspiring villains at Duel of Death, to justice.

Which wouldn't happen. Not if Manager Liang had been passing off silver taels to Magistrate Ho—she was almost certain of it. Liang's riches might rival Merchant Guo's, if only one knew all of his assets, and he certainly was not above bribing. In fact, she had done some bribing herself—small amounts of course—when necessary.

If the officials were corrupt, then it was her job to bring justice. Old Man Liu had made it clear to her that she was trained for this purpose, in an era when the common folk suffered and those in power were rotten. Even though Duel of Death was no picnic—that night of spying had taught her much—she would arm herself with as many weapons and gadgets as possible, and do away with the people who ought to lay down their lives for poisoning another.

Her decision made, Hong finally fell asleep.

The next day, Hong rose earlier than usual. Since Governor Shue was still on his way to the capital, she had less to do. After cleaning the furniture in her master's room, she told the elderly servant that she had to visit her *sifu*. Since Meng-Ting had been arrested, it was natural that she wanted to inform and comfort Old Man Liu, so the servant didn't complain.

She hurried to the stables. Today she did not want to walk; a donkey would get her to her *sifu* sooner. When she passed by Fang's steed, she felt a pang of agony. The steed, a handsome breed bought from the Uighurs in northwestern China, had its head down and its eyelids half closed, as though it were lonely.

"Don't brood," Hong told the horse. "I will save your master and bring him home."

"Miss Hong?" The Turk who cared for the horses stood over her. "I've been hearing that Young Master Fang is still in prison. Has a verdict been issued?"

"No. But he is still in jail." Hong swung on top of the donkey. "I am going to ask for help. If I am not back for lunch, do not be worried. I will be at my *sifu's*."

"I get your message. Good luck, Miss Hong."

The exterior doors of Old Man Liu's compound had been left open. Hong didn't even have to knock. She went straight in—and halted.

Next to her *sifu* was a young man. He was rather nice-looking, with large limpid eyes and delicate features that gave him an almost feminine appearance. While his hands were covered with blisters and bruises from work, his face spoke otherwise. At sight of her, he gave her a small smile, though a shade of sadness hung over him.

"Meng-Chou?" Hong said. She hadn't seen him for weeks. Meng-Chou, the younger brother of Meng-Ting, worked as a carpenter in a remote corner of the city. Besides his normal work of fashioning tables and chairs, he also designed many weapons for Hong. Old Man Liu would suggest or even draw the design, and Hong would convey those to Meng-Chou, on the pretence that Liu wanted some handicraft from his other grandson.

"Naturally he'd be here," Old Man Liu snapped. "What is this I'm hearing of—Meng-Ting also in jail?"

"It was Manager Liang and his cronies." Hong clenched her fists. "They accused Meng-Ting of supplying the poison that killed Yao. By some despicable means, they stole Three-Steps-to-Hell from his store, and used it to cover up their plan of poisoning their own fighter."

"They did?" Meng-Chou said.

"I heard it with my own ears." Hong told them of the night she had spied on Manager Liang. "Meng-Chou, can you fashion me some new weapons? I want to find an appropriate time to sneak into Duel of Death and deal justice to those who committed the crime."

"There is no need," Old Man Liu said sharply.

"But *sifu,* the magistrate won't listen…"

"You want to deal justice to the one who poisoned Yao? Fine. Do you even know who it is?"

"Whirlwind Ko. Potbelly. Or even Manager Liang."

"You're wrong."

The abrupt, harsh tone of her *sifu* startled her.

"Hong," Meng-Chou said gently. "Have you considered that it would be strange for the manager to kill his prized fighter? Especially when Yao was bringing in so much money?"

Hong paused. "It could be Ko. Mrs. Yao told me he was nicknamed Second Man, meaning he always came second to Yao. Perhaps Ko always wanted to get rid of the person who has bested him?"

"Pure speculation. Have you even met this Ko?" Old Man Liu said, shaking his head. "All right, suppose it is him. You storm into Duel of Death and kill this Ko. Would that cause the magistrate to pardon Fang?"

Hong was silent. Her *sifu* was right. How could she be so dense, so irrational? Obviously, her concern for Fang had clouded her mind.

"As a matter of fact," Old Man Liu said. "We have already found out who supplied the poison. It was not someone in Duel of Death."

"Impossible. I heard it myself."

"Manager Liang merely wanted to *drug* Yao; he only wanted to weaken his fighter. Now, the poison used is uncommonly lethal. Meng-Ting said that Three-Steps-To Hell was only used when ending the suffering of a chronically ill patient, or someone who is injured far too seriously."

Old Man Liu folded his hands and leaned forward.

"Hong, it's the child Meng-Ting employed. Ah-Ming swapped the drug for the poison. Ah-Ming was the one who poisoned Yao."

Hong felt as though the world had turned over.

"A... Ah-Ming?" she whispered. The poor child wouldn't harm a fly! But then... considering that Yao had killed his father and no attempt was made to arrest him, there was the motive. And since Ah-Ming was also helping out at Meng-Ting's...

"I don't believe it," she said, but her voice sounded empty.

"Ah-Ming came to us when Meng-Ting didn't return to the store," Meng-Chou said quietly. "When he learnt that Meng-Ting was arrested, the poor child broke down and told us everything. He happened to overhear the people from Duel of Death talking when they came to buy drugs. He saw his chance. When

Meng-Ting called him to wrap up the order, he slipped in Three-Steps-to-Hell instead. Meng-Ting never missed it; he rarely used that poison unless necessary."

"So what do you say, huh?" Old Man Liu said. "Going to turn in Ah-Ming to the magistrate?"

Hong wrung her hands. What Ah-Ming had done was not something she would encourage, but nevertheless understandable. Children were always expected to avenge their parents—it was in the teachings of Confucius.

If only she had reached Yao first!

"I... can't," she finally said. "Is there a way to save Master Fang and Meng-Ting without sacrificing the child?"

"I thought you'd say that," Old Man Liu said. "Now, I wouldn't recommend going off to kill those bastards at Duel of Death. Heaven knows how many nefarious deeds they've done, but as long as they don't do something that'll warrant a death sentence, we'll leave them alone. What I would suggest is that you try to save Meng-Ting. Go to the prison and figure out how to get him out. He can leave the city and find business elsewhere. An apothecary isn't a noble profession, but people are always in need of one."

Meng-Chou started. "Grandfather, are you certain? Are you meaning to send Meng-Ting on the run?"

"What about Master Fang?" Hong said.

"If you have a better plan, then tell me. Magistrate Ho doesn't care who did it, as long as he finds someone," Old Man Liu said. "As for the Fang kid, they won't really execute him. He is the son of the governor, and even though Ho isn't afraid of Shue Song, he wouldn't want to be on his bad side either. I dare say he'll keep Fang in jail as long as the kid admits his guilt. Then Ho will say that since Fang has shown remorse, he will subject him to a hundred lashings only. The kid will be set free, eventually."

A hundred lashings! As much as she believed in Fang's body strength, a hundred lashings would still easily render him bloody and unconscious.

"So what do you say, Hong?" Old Man Liu looked at her expectantly.

Hong straightened her shoulders.

"I'll do it."

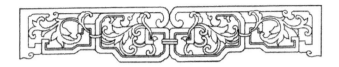

20

A desolate atmosphere still hung over the house when Hong returned. Only two days remained until the second hearing.

Hong went to the kitchen. Golden Lotus happened to be packing up a food basket for Fang.

"I will go with you." Hong washed two pairs of chopsticks and laid them in the basket. "Do you mind if I pack some food for Mr. Liu as well? *Sifu* wanted me to bring lunch for him."

"Hong." Golden Lotus fixed her with a piercing gaze. "Is it because of Mr. Liu Meng-Ting that you are refusing Master Fang?"

"It has nothing to do with him," Hong said calmly. "I am going to see him just because *sifu* asked me to. I'll say this—Mr. Liu and I are only friends. By the way, have the other young masters decided how to save Master Fang?"

"We tried eavesdropping last night, Silver Peony and I. Master Gwang was in favour of bribing the magistrate so Master Fang wouldn't suffer. Master

Ping preferred to continue finding a way to prove Master Fang's innocence. But when they discovered us listening, they shooed us away so I don't know what they eventually decided to do." Golden Lotus sighed. "So far, all evidence still points to Master Fang! Oh, *why* did he choose to go to see that damned fighter that day?"

An hour later, they arrived at the magistrate's tribunal.

"We'd like to see Master Shue Fang and Mr. Liu," Hong told the jailer. "We are from the governor's house." As was the unspoken custom, she slipped a piece of silver in his hand. "You must have a load of work guarding, so here's a little compensation. Buy a cool drink or something."

"Ah…" The jailer pocketed the money willingly. His gaze roved over her face, then settled on Golden Lotus, whose beauty and youth was like a beacon of light in the gloomy, smelly prison. "What's your name, girlie?"

Golden Lotus shrank back. Normally she was blithe and bold, but the jailer was a rather nasty-looking personage with all of his teeth missing except for one large tooth.

"She is one of Governor Shue's servants," Hong quickly said, hoping that the mention of the governor would daunt the jailer. "She has been held very favourably in his regard."

The jailer licked his lips. Finally he decided that it wasn't worth his time to take advantage of Golden Lotus. "A favourite, eh? Not surprised." He took a bunch of keys from a drawer. "Follow me."

It was a dusty, murky place, reeking with the smell of sweat and urine. A few prisoners lay in their

176

cells, oblivious to the outside world, but others made catcalls and leered at Hong and Golden Lotus. Hong made sure that her needles and darts were well within reach. Were she ever to visit a prison cell again, she would do well to don a disguise.

Fang had a single cell for himself, courtesy of being the governor's son. When Hong and Golden Lotus approached, he sprang out of the straw bed.

"What are you doing here?" he said, his voice low and urgent. "This is no fit place for you girls!"

"Master!" Golden Lotus promptly burst into tears. "You… it must be awful, dreadful, terrible for you…"

He did look like he had lost a good amount of weight. His eyes were bloodshot, his hair was unkempt, his white linen prison uniform was coarse and filthy. He looked nothing like the handsome young man who had attracted the fancy of the Queen of Flowers.

Hong stayed calm. "We wanted to see you. Golden Lotus, the sweets?"

"Oh yes." Golden Lotus quickly dried her tears. "Here you are, Young Master, all your favourites: plum cake, almond cake, and red bean cake."

"Young Master," Hong continued. "We've been trying to find the real killer to clear your name. Unfortunately, it isn't going as well as we hoped. Before you landed in jail," she lowered her voice, "did you manage to find anything?"

Fang thought for a while. He relayed to her some facts, but nothing that she hadn't heard before, such as Opal's concealed debts and Yao's relationship with her.

"Oh! Does that mean you'll eventually have to... have to..." Golden Lotus looked on the verge of crying again.

"Don't worry about me," Fang said bravely. "It isn't that bad living here—well, it is pretty bad—but I'm sure they won't order my head. They just need to keep me inside because the magistrate's son hates me, and to let the public know that the magistrate has been doing his job."

"But you're innocent," Golden Lotus cried. "I just know you are."

"I am not going to give up," Hong said firmly. "We will all make every effort to exonerate you. Young Master, you deserve better than to be used for spite."

She met his eyes squarely, and was half-gratified, half-dismayed to see the passion in his gaze. Were it not for the presence of others, and the fact that he was wearing filthy clothes in a filthy cell, she was pretty sure that he would have caught her in his arms and kissed her.

Which she wouldn't mind, actually. But there were more pressing matters on hand.

"I have to see Meng-Ting as well," she finally said, touching his elbow lightly. "*Sifu* made me promise to see to his meals."

A slight look of disappointment crossed Fang's face, but he nodded. "Go to the second last cell. And Hong, you'll come visit again, won't you?"

"I will."

With a final gaze at her young master, Hong proceeded to Meng-Ting's cell. Unlike Fang, Meng-Ting did not have the luxury of having a room of his own. Three other prisoners shared his cell.

Fortunately, they had been in prison too long and were too lethargic to hurl offensive remarks.

"Are you all right?" Hong said anxiously. It wasn't long that Meng-Ting had been arrested, but already he looked terrible in the prisoner's clothes of rough material. He looked dishevelled and starved.

"Awful. Dreadful. Please, give me one of my own poisonous pills so I can die."

When Hong raised her eyebrows, Meng-Ting smiled. "The thought has crossed my mind, but I'm feeling a lot better now that you've arrived. Ooh, is that a roast chicken leg? I don't even recall eating this well in my prison-less days."

"Thank Young Master Fang," Hong said. "The maids have been spending a lot more time in the kitchens so they can make sure he doesn't starve."

"Lucky him," Meng-Ting grinned, tearing off some meat. When he finished the chicken, colour returned to his face. "I'm glad you came," he repeated, though this time he lowered his voice. "You see, I've been hoping you could look into this issue. I managed to talk a bit with Fang before we got separated, and there's something about the poisoning that strikes me as peculiar."

"What do you mean?"

"Fang tells me that there was a wine jar on the table when he found Yao. He had assumed Yao was poisoned by the wine—after all, the man was known to be a heavy drinker and is dangerously violent when he's drunk. Three-Steps-to-Hell may be as transparent as water, but it tastes extremely bitter. I can't believe that anyone would keep on drinking the wine when the taste is drastically changed."

Hong pursed her lips. "Would it be possible that when Yao tasted the bitterness he stopped drinking, but the one sip he took was powerful enough to kill him?"

"Then he should have spat out the wine, like all over the floor, but Fang said there was no trace of any spilt wine. Besides, if Yao spat out the wine, then the little poison he had should not have killed him. A baby, maybe, but definitely not a big, strong fighter. The most the poison would have done was to render him unconscious. Kind of odd, as I see it."

Hong turned the matter over her head. Could it be—could it be that someone else had killed Yao when the poison had proved ineffective? Maybe Whirlwind Ko had come to check Yao's condition, and upon finding the star fighter weakened and unconscious, decided to do away the man who prevented him receiving the number one title?

"I'll go question the coroner," she said.

"Be quick! I'll perish if I continue to stay in this hell hole!"

Once Hong and Golden Lotus departed, Fang sank on the cold, hard stone floor. The bed provided wasn't much better—the blanket was flimsy and ragged and had numerous holes and tears. Goodness knows how many unwashed, unkempt prisoners had used it before him. Yet, no matter how much the blanket repulsed him, he had to use it every time he slept, when frigid night air seeped in through the prison bars and the threadbare prison uniform he wore couldn't keep his teeth from chattering.

It was miserable enough, but what worried him more was what fate awaited him. His father was still at the capital, and his brothers and sister so far had little success in getting him out. Even though he was certain that his life would not be forfeited, he had no idea what the magistrate would decide eventually. Unless they found the real murderer, it was unlikely he'd be let go without some form of punishment.

Fang shivered. The basket that Golden Lotus and Hong brought still sat in a corner. Hong… how relieved he was that she didn't recoil at his frightful appearance. She had looked at him with compassion, touched him without hesitation, and told him that she believed in him. Even if she hadn't shown any romantic feelings for him yet, there was hope that he could make her love him. Already he missed her presence.

There was the sound of keys jingling and footsteps approaching.

Fang couldn't believe it… did Hong suddenly return?

But his hopes were shattered. Ho Jiang-Min, the one person he possibly detested most in the world, was looking down at him, his expression smug.

"Master Ho, are you sure you want to enter the cell?" the jailer asked, in an ingratiating, sycophantic manner. "The interior is too dirty for the soles of your shoes."

"It'll only be a minute," Jiang-Min replied, smirking. "I couldn't exactly pass up a chance to re-acquaint myself with the *noble* governor's son, could I?"

The jailor let out a chuckle, though his voice was wary when he spoke. "Well, let me know immediately if you need anything, Master Ho, if the prisoner gets out of hand…"

The smirk vanished. "Are you saying that I can't handle a handcuffed man on my own?"

"No! Of course not, my deepest apologies, sir, I'll just go." And the jailor disappeared, leaving Fang and Jiang-Min alone.

"My, my." Jiang-Min shook his head. "Not as cocky as we're used to, eh? The chains on your wrists made a dent on your arrogance, eh?"

Fang remained stoic. He could attack Jiang-Min if he wanted, but he knew well the consequences.

"Hmm. I take back my words—you are still as arrogant as usual." Jiang-Min scowled. "You know, Fang, you've always annoyed me. We aren't that different—about the same age and have a good standing, yet you flaunt your noble character as if I am the scoundrel."

Fang still didn't speak, nor acknowledge his presence.

"Quit pretending, you bastard!" Jiang-Min snarled, and pounded on the door with a fist. "You could have the time of your life—women, wine, wealth, anything! But you insist on being so disgustingly self-righteous—is it going to earn you a plaque, huh?"

Jiang-Min breathed hard, his chest heaving up and down. "You ought to be grateful, now that I am offering you a proposition. I can get you out of this cell, as long as you agree to my terms."

Fang finally looked up. He still held nothing but contempt for the magistrate's son, but at the same time, he couldn't help wondering what proposition Jiang-Min had in mind.

"That maid of yours who just came to visit—Golden Lotus is her name, huh? She seems pretty attached to you." Jiang-Min smiled nastily. "From that look of her, she's still a fresh young maiden. If you give her to me, I'll see that you're freed at once."

Fang stood up. His eyes blazed.

"No way."

"What?" Jiang-Min looked flabbergasted. "You have scores of girls at home, and you can't even yield one for your freedom? "

"None of my servants are to be given away like cattle on the market," Fang said firmly. "Especially not to vermin like you."

Infuriated, Jiang-Min kicked him in the stomach—hard. Taken by surprise, and also weakened by his stay in the prison, Fang failed to dodge in time. He doubled up in pain, only to be hit again—this time on his shins, making him fall on the floor. Jiang-Min stepped on his hand, grinding his boot into Fang's palm.

"Self-righteous prick," he hissed, his voice dripping with venom. "I have given you a chance. I was lenient. Since you want to play the hero," he stomped on Fang's hand, and the latter bit his lip to keep from yelping in pain, "then have it your way. Don't think your family can save you. Old Shue may be the governor, but the emperor is my brother-in-law. You'll never compete with that. Ever."

He finished with a final kick on Fang's face, driving his head on the hard stone floor. Blood trickled down the side of his face. How he wished he could fight back, but his body was still in pain from the kicking and his hands were chained.

"Hmph." Jiang-Min spat on his hair. "You look a complete wreck. Let's see if your pretty little maid'll still care for you when she comes next time."

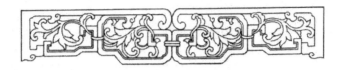

21

Hong found it hard to find the time to seek the coroner once she had returned from Old Man Liu's. Now that the maids were pouring their energy into cooking for Fang and preparing other necessities he might need in prison, they neglected their duties. The cook became cranky, and so did the laundress, and even the elder brothers were displeased when their rooms were not cleaned every day.

"Girl!" the cook barked. "Are you going out *again?*"

"Er... I..."

"You have been gone for half the day! Are you a servant here or do I have to come and serve *you* now? Clear away the dirty dishes and wash them!"

Hong swallowed her desire to go out. Crossing over to the table, she picked up the dishes.

"Those maids," the cook grumbled. "How many of them are now packing food baskets? We have other people in the family!"

Silently, Hong washed and cleaned. She could hear the cook's complaints but she did not take them to heart. While she smiled and nodded like a mechanical object, her mind was wandering elsewhere.

If what Meng-Ting said was true—and she trusted him, so it *must* be true—she might have the chance to accuse Duel of Death of lying. If Three-Steps-to-Hell was not the cause of Yao's death, then Manager Liang and Potbelly's statement that Fang and Meng-Ting had worked together to poison Yao was false—deliberately so. But to expose them of lying, she had to get the coroner to give the evidence first.

In the afternoon, Hong slipped out of the compound. Fortunately at this time, most of the higher-ranked servants were resting, leaving a few lower-ranked ones doing menial work.

She knew that finding the coroner's place and interrogating him would take some time, so she decided to use someone else to ask for her. Hong found her target sitting cross-legged at one of the streets near Heavenly Pleasures. It was one of the beggar spies whom her *sifu* employed.

"Good afternoon," Hong murmured, barely looking at the beggar. "I've something to ask of you."

The beggar smiled. "Anything, anything! Please, give this unworthy one something so he may not starve."

Hong bent down and placed two coppers in his begging bowl. At the same time, she managed to shove a folded piece of paper in his lap, which included her instructions.

"This is half the payment up front," she whispered. "You shall receive the other half when you accomplish what I ask. I'll be back tomorrow at the same time."

She left abruptly, hoping that she had chosen well. The beggar had had his fingers chopped off in a previous job, but he had developed adroitness with his legs and moreover, he was not deaf. If everything went well, she would have her information the following day.

The beggar proved to be efficient. When Hong went to seek him the next day, he feigned an excessive amount of gladness at her altruism, and gave her the info on the same piece of paper.

Hong ducked in a small alley, unfolded the paper, and began to read. The beggar's writing was atrocious, since he wrote with his right foot, but she had been communicating long enough with him to distinguish his "foot-writing" well enough.

What she learnt made her decide to visit Old Man Liu immediately.

"*Sifu*," Hong said, holding out the paper. "This is what I have asked one of your spies to find out."

"What is this?" Old Man Liu grunted.

"What the coroner had actually found out when performing the autopsy on Yao. He wasn't poisoned. At all. The wine jar containing the poison was untouched. Yao was probably killed before he had a chance to tear off the paper cap on the jar."

Old Man Liu, who was holding a cup of tea, paused.

"Not poisoned, you say? Then what was the cause?"

"He says that there's a purple bruise on Yao's chest, the shape of a hand print. His inner organs are ruptured, but no bones are broken. "

Splash! The tea cup Old Man Liu was holding fell on the ground, shattering into several pieces and drenching the hem of his robe.

Immediately, Hong knelt and picked up the pieces, berating herself for not acting faster.

"I'll go get a cloth," she said, meaning to clean up the soaked material of his robe, but Liu reached out and gripped her elbow firmly.

"The Lost Manual," he rasped. "It's *the Lost Manual*! Someone has obviously used the power as dictated. That's why that Yao was so easily defeated."

"*Sifu*," Hong began, feeling alarmed. When Old Man Liu had mentioned the Lost Manual, she had assumed it a legend, a story that was more fiction than fact. "You said that the Lost Manual has not been seen for twenty years. For all we know, there may be other forms of martial arts that can cause inner damage."

The elderly man made a noise of impatience. "Tut, tut, you are still ignorant of the world of fighting arts! Did you not say that Yao is the best fighter in the city? That his body showed no trace of struggle, or resistance? Only a legendary work like the Lost Manual can deliver a fighting art powerful enough to defeat a brilliant fighter like that."

He loosened Hong's elbow. "Girlie, now is our chance. *Find out who killed Yao.*"

A chill ran down Hong's spine.

"*Sifu*, are you certain it is really the Lost Manual?"

"Meng-Ting told you that Yao couldn't have consumed Three-Steps-to-Hell, didn't he? If not for the Lost Manual, what could have killed Yao?"

Hong kept silent, not wanting to argue. How far-fetched the idea sounded! Theoretically, it *was* possible. But Old Man Liu hadn't even *seen* the body. How could he simply make a judgement based on what the coroner had said? Furthermore, even if what he guessed was true, how was she going to find the murderer?

"Tell Meng-Chou to fashion a new weapon for you. Something that's truly fast and unexpected. That murderer with the Lost Manual is no picnic—he may possibly be the worst enemy you come across! When I asked you to do away with Yao, I already had some worries, since all the victims you have dealt with knew little about martial arts. But now things are different. One blow from the killer, and you're dead."

"I will do my best with the weapons." Hong tried not to let fear seep into her tone. Even if it wasn't the Lost Manual, there was no question that the murderer possessed deadly skills.

"Go and find Meng-Chou," Old Man Liu ordered. "Ask him if he still has those hollowed pens."

"Hollowed pens?"

Meng-Chou lived in a secluded part of town, away in a narrow alley. Few people actually passed by his shop unless they deliberately sought him. In this aspect, he was more similar to his grandfather, preferring peace and quiet as he worked as a carpenter. His handmade crafts were few but exquisitely made, earning a reputation among those who appreciated quality woodwork. Somehow the remoteness of his place did not deter customers.

When Hong arrived, she found the shop empty. It was kept scrupulously clean for a man who lived by himself—Meng-Chou was the only man she knew who maintained such cleanliness. Only a small child sat in the shop, playing with a spinning top.

"Hello, Little One," Hong said. She recognised the child as Ah-Mei, the eighth child of a big family. Ah-Mei was neglected often, so she preferred to come over to Meng-Chou's and play. "Is Mr. Liu working in the back?"

"Right-o, Miss Hong." Ah-Mei jumped up and bowed, almost comically.

Hong smiled and patted her head. "What a pretty top. Did Mr. Liu make that for you?"

Ah-Mei nodded fervently. "Mr. Liu is so clever! I want to marry him when I grow up!"

Hong laughed. "Then you have made a good start."

She went out through the side door and into the back yard, where Meng-Chou was bent over a table, industriously carving a statue. Unlike Old Man Liu, however, Meng-Chou was never an astute listener. He was often so absorbed in his work that Hong had to say his name twice to get his attention.

Today, she simply plucked a tiny stone from the ground and flicked it. The stone whizzed through the air and landed on the table, inches from the statue.

Meng-Chou turned around. A soft smile lightened up his face.

"Hong." Slowly, he put down his statue. "A pleasant surprise."

"*Sifu* sent me."

"Is there news about my brother?"

Hong quickly related what Meng-Ting told her, plus Old Man Liu's instructions.

"He told me to fashion you another weapon?"

"Hollowed pens. He said you'd know."

Meng-Chou raised an eyebrow. "It has been some time since I made those. Grandfather had said he preferred flying weapons that demonstrated skill of the person, not of the weapon itself."

Hong was intrigued. "Show me."

Meng-Chou dusted his hands and rose from his work bench. "I believe I still have some in storage. Has Ah-Mei served you tea?"

"No, but that is all right. Your tea is terrible. Master Liu would certainly disown you if you served him tea with sawdust floating on top."

Meng-Chou smiled. He led the way to a small shed in the yard. When he emerged from the shed, he carried a long ebony box. In the box lay several pens, all fashioned from high-quality bamboo.

"There is a switch." Meng-Chou turned a pen in his palm, the brush end facing him, while the other end pointed to a tree. "Watch."

He pressed a spot on the pen, and a long silver needle shot out, embedding itself in the tree.

"The mechanism is powered by springs." Meng-Chou turned the pen over and showed her the hollowed inside. "Just press—and the needle comes out. No one will ever notice that you're carrying a deadly weapon."

Hong took the pen and felt the smooth bamboo, cool against her skin.

"Amazing design," she murmured.

"Grandfather used to carry them when he was working at the palace," Meng-Chou said. "But he doesn't use them very often. He's worried that someone might discover the secret of the pens and so the work will be copied." He tested the pens on the wall and found three of them worked well. Still, he brought a tube of oil and fixed them all.

Again, Hong thought about asking of Old Man Liu's past, the time when he had worked in the palace as of the musicians, but she said nothing. Despite claiming her as a disciple and instructing her in the art of weaponry, Old Man Liu never brought up his past, at least not when it was connected with his days at the imperial court.

"There." Meng-Chou handed her the pens. "The mechanism will make it easier to hit your target. The tiny needles and darts you usually carry are more difficult if you're surrounded by multiple opponents and cannot aim carefully."

"It's a skill I've yet to master," Hong admitted ruefully. "*Sifu* can shoot ten darts and all ten hit the mark, even when he's talking to me, but I can't. I can have perfect aim, but only when I'm fully concentrating."

"Still, it's impressive what you have done so far." Meng-Chou smiled affectionately at her. "When Grandfather started training you, Meng-Ting and I had doubts, because you were originally from a wealthy family. We weren't sure if you could withstand the training, when none of us could."

"*Sifu* may be blind in body, but his mind is sharper than any of us," Hong said. "He sensed from my talk, my movements, that I could be a worthy disciple to him."

"Be extra careful this time," Meng-Chou said. "If someone with the legendary ability of the Lost Manual has killed Yao, he must not be underestimated. Are your other weapons all right? Any sharpening or polishing needed?"

"Several of my darts are getting blunt with use," Hong admitted.

When Meng-Chou was done fixing her weapons, he again bade her to be careful.

"I shouldn't doubt your ability, but from what I've heard from Grandfather, this time is different. None of your previous opponents were skilled in martial arts. If what Grandfather said of the Lost Manual is true…"

"I can do this," Hong said firmly. "Meng-Ting and Master Fang are suffering in jail. I *have* to bring this matter to an end."

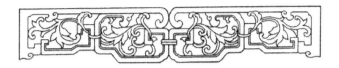

22

On her way home, Hong noticed a crowd gathered in a circle. A simple stall was set up nearby; two queues of a total of twenty or more people were waiting at the stall. A glance told Hong that the queue consisted of people who had more or less training in martial arts, either from the way they positioned themselves or the manner they talked. Interestingly, the two queues were divided by gender: one queue consisted of men, the other of women.

She tapped one of the onlookers in the crowd.

"Pardon me, but can you tell me what's going on?"

"Merchant Guo is hiring more bodyguards, missus! He's offering a thousand silver taels for anyone who can beat the five bodyguards he has here."

Hong strove to stand on tiptoe, but too many people blocked her view. However, she could distinctly hear the sound of fists hitting flesh. Since the crowd was practically quiet, the fight must be intense.

"Do you know why he's hiring?"

"Seems like his place got robbed." The man shrugged. "No surprises there; Merchant Guo's the richest person in town."

Hong remembered last time when they visited the Guo residence. Mrs. Guo had mentioned robbers infiltrating the place. It seemed that Merchant Guo was over-reacting; not only was he hiring bodyguards to protect his treasury, but also to protect the women of the household.

"But I know how to fight!" a voice came from the head of the queue. It was a scrawny-looking young man dressed in a tattered grey robe.

"That ain't enough, youngster," a man at the recruiting stall said. "We're paying good money for this job, we don't bother with people who aren't taller than my shoulder."

"But I've won fights against people who're bigger than me!" the young man said. "This ain't a fair duel between fighters, I know how to take advantage in a fight. Trust me, you won't regret hiring me. What about those women, hey?" He gestured toward the other queue. "They aren't the least intimidating!"

"Don't question me on our master's orders," the recruiter said with a scowl. "Since you are male, only those who fulfil size requirements can enter."

The young man looked sullen. Suddenly, he lashed out at the man, catching him by the ankle.

The recruiter, caught off guard, was flipped over his shoulder.

"Hey!" the other recruiters shouted. "Get off, you impudent scoundrel! Don't ever show your face again!"

"I beat him!" the young man insisted. "Didn't you just see? I beat him!"

While the stall erupted in chaos, Hong walked away. The requirements were understandable for some, but for real martial artists, it *was* true that smaller opponents could win. During her own experience of dealing with larger opponents, she found she could easily gain the upper hand through agility and reflexes. Not to mention that the flying weapons helped.

"Why, if it isn't Miss Hong."

It was a young, pretty servant maid with two braids curled and twisted on both of sides of her head.

"Little Jade?" Hong said. "Are you on an errand?"

Little Jade nodded, showing her basket filled with soy sauce jars and bean curd wrapped in oil paper. "For my mistress; recently she has been really stressed. Ever since the day of the outing—I guess she doesn't feel like risking it. You know, the baby." She sighed, her eyes darting towards the crowd around the competing bodyguards. "You saw us recruiting more bodyguards, no? My mistress specifically requested female bodyguards for her protection. I mean, anything can happen if a thief makes a wrong turn and ends up at her residence quarters."

"Mrs. Guo is stressed about potential robberies?" Hong said.

"Oh, she's totally freaked out over it!" Little Jade said, shaking her head. "She's become paranoid, I tell you. Like, when the wind blows on the bamboo curtain and makes this tiny noise, she jumps. I don't know why she's so agitated—I mean, I know she's worried about the baby, but this isn't healthy for the baby either."

Hong remembered the couple of times they'd seen Mrs. Guo since her marriage. She did seem extremely cautious to protect her baby. And although Hong had never troubled herself with child-bearing, she knew that it was vital for a married woman to produce an heir and continue her husband's bloodline.

"By the way, how is Master Fang doing?" Little Jade went on. "I'm so sorry that he was accused of having a liaison with Opal. Which is so untrue! I've been wanting to sail over to the magistrate myself and plead clemency for Master Fang, but he would never listen to a lowly servant like me. He doesn't even listen to his own daughter!"

Opal. Hong hadn't thought much about Opal before. Come to think of it, Fang's going to see Yao *was* to do with Opal's death…

"Little Jade, you knew Opal, right? She was killed before Yao. Have you any thought who might have killed her?"

"Well…" Little Jade shivered. "I don't really know. Opal was four years my senior; she used to be Mistress Guo's personal handmaid before she married. I assumed that Yao would have killed Opal, because they were once lovers, but Opal went off and married another man. But since Yao also died, I… I can't think of anyone specific."

She spoke slowly, in a way that reminded Hong of Golden Lotus. Golden Lotus usually spoke in that tone when she was revealing less than she knew, even though she wasn't lying.

"If not someone specific, then what might be possible for causing Opal's death? Other than Yao's jealousy?"

"Well…" Little Jade bit her lip. "I don't feel like speaking ill of the dead…"

"Little Jade." Hong fixed her with a steadfast gaze. "Master Fang is in jail. Is it not more important to do your best to save the living instead?"

"All right, but I really don't know that much. I'm just guessing. Opal used to be in debt. Huge debts that we weren't able to help her with. But somehow, she managed to pay them off. We didn't know where the money came from. My guess is that she got mixed up with a bad crowd. Maybe Yao was involved as well, they were always pretty close. So when she ditched him and got married, I think she wanted to start over with a new life. But she still had something unsettled with the shady people, so they came back to kill her and Yao. It's all guesswork, though. You can ask Opal's family, they should be able to tell you more than I know."

Could it be Madam Jin from Heavenly Pleasures? Hong remembered when Fang had gone to see Madam Jin and paid her five hundred taels. Was he paying Opal's debt? If Little Jade guessed right, who had actually killed Opal and Yao? Someone like Madam Jin could certainly afford to pay for a killer powerful enough to murder Yao without using poison. In fact, if she narrowed down the suspects by their ability to pay a huge sum of money… *only a few in the city would qualify*.

She needed more information.

"Please tell me Opal's family's address."

Little Jade named a place in the northwest part of the city. When Hong thanked her and turned to leave, Little Jade suddenly caught her sleeve.

"What you're doing—it's dangerous, you know? You really like Master Fang, don't you?"

Hong hesitated. It would be so easy to lie, to say that she was merely doing this because he was her master. Shu-Mo was likely to do the same. But she didn't want to feign indifference. She would be leaving soon, anyway.

"I do," she said, smiling.

"Oh…" Little Jade drew a deep breath. "Best of luck, then. Master Fang is a lucky man!"

Unsurprisingly, Opal's family was located in one of the rundown areas of the city. Hong could feel the eyes of children and elderly on her as she walked past. Her heart ached, but there was little she could do.

"I'd like to see Mr. Kwang's house," she said, giving a copper to a beggar.

"Mr. Kwang? He died a few years ago. A good-for-nothing, all he did was gamble and pile up debts. Got into a drunken brawl and had a blow that cracked his ribs."

"How about the rest of his family? Are they still living around here?"

"Widow and a son," the beggar said. "Go down this street and turn at the donkey cart. House has some calligraphy hung over the door."

Hong thanked him and went to look for the Kwang residence.

When she reached the house, she found a young man dozing on a bamboo chair outside. A scroll of the Analects on a small table lay open before him.

Hong rapped on the table. He slowly opened his eyes.

"Hello," she said politely. "My name is Hong and I work at the governor's house. Are you a relative of Kwang Opal?"

"Why yes," the young man stammered. Realising that he had drooled when he slept, he quickly swiped his face with his sleeve. "I am her younger brother, Kwang Lo-Wei. What can I do for you?"

"May we speak inside?" Hong lowered her voice. "I have come to enquire about your sister's death."

Lo-Wei stared. "Wait. You said you are from the governor's? Or was it the magistrate's?"

"The governor. Mr. Chow works at the governor's."

"Oh, right." Lo-Wei jumped up. He pushed the door open and led her inside. The interior was neat but sparse.

"Mother!" he called. "We have a visitor!"

A middle-aged woman came out. Though her face and body matched her age, streaks of white and silver peppered her hair.

"Who are you?" she asked. Her eyes darted around nervously. "Are you—are you from the magistrate's house?"

Hong repeated what she had told Lo-Wei. "Madam, please forgive me for this sudden visit, but I would like to find out who was responsible for your daughter's death."

Mrs. Kwang twisted her hands and her expression became quite wild. "Oh, my poor Opal. I truly thought that she'd be happy and well off when she married. When she... passed away, I didn't think it was possible. Even the debt collectors... we were almost finished with them..."

"Did those debt collectors threaten you?" Hong said.

"N... no, but they warned Opal that they'd want her to work at the brothel if she failed to pay up."

"How much did you owe?"

"Two thousand taels of silver," Lo-Wei supplied, keeping his head down in shame. "It was Pa's fault—he couldn't stop going to the gamblers."

"Don't speak of your father in that disrespectful tone," Mrs. Kwang said sharply. Although she appeared meek, she was quick to admonish her son. "He's in the grave now—may he rest in peace!"

Hong turned the matter over her mind. "But your daughter was only a servant maid. Even after marriage, she couldn't possibly raise enough to pay off a two-thousand-tael debt."

"The magistrate's daughter bestowed on her some worthy gifts," Mrs. Kwang said.

"Valuable scrolls of serious poetry," Lo-Wei put in. "The prefaces had genuine handwriting from a couple of famous poets. Guess the magistrate's daughter didn't care for those."

Hong frowned. She distinctly remembered Little Jade saying that Opal hadn't accepted anything from the magistrate's daughter. Where had Opal procured those scrolls of poetry?

"May I see the scrolls?"

"We sold them all," Mrs. Kwang said, shrugging. "We just had enough left over for Lo-Wei. He needs the travel expenses for the scholar examinations in the capital. He... he's quite industrious, you see." She looked pointedly at Hong, as though hoping Hong would look more favourably on her son.

"There was something funny about the scrolls, though," Lo-Wei said. "One of them had a piece of paper wedged in it. There was a love poem on the paper—I think it was addressed to the magistrate's daughter."

"Do you have the poem?"

"Oh, I returned it to Opal, it shouldn't belong here. But I can still remember it—

Your eyes shine more beautifully than the diamonds on your throat,

Your skin glows brighter than the pearls you wear,
Your beauty is so natural, so alluring, so bewitching,
My heart is forever yours, maiden so fair."

Hong wrinkled her brow. She had not read much poetry, but the lines she had just heard were simply atrocious. Surely it could not have been the work of Mr. Guo.

She decided to pay a visit to Mrs. Guo. Perhaps the magistrate's daughter could shed some more light on her former maid.

"Thank you very much," she said, bowing. "I will let you know if I find anything."

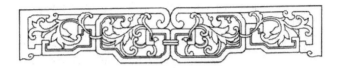

23

The first thing that Hong noticed about the Guo residence was the number of guards at the entrance had dramatically increased. Last time, there had been four burly, bear-resembling, menacing guards, who only softened at sight of Golden Lotus. Today, there were ten burly, bear-resembling guards, of whom nine out of ten only glanced casually at her plain blue robes and resumed their door-guarding duties. The remaining one came up to her and said with a resigned sigh, "What do you want?"

"I am from the governor's household," Hong said carefully. "I have been here before, in the company of my mistress, Lady Lynn."

The other guard looked bored. Probably he had been asked to stand here all day. Then suddenly, recognition dawned on his face.

"Ah, you are the maid who visited last time? There was this other girl, the one with flowery skirts…"

"Golden Lotus," Hong supplied. "Yes, I work with her. We all belong to the Shue household. In fact, if you could summon Little Jade, she will recognise me."

"Oh, come on, old Hu!" the first guard said. "Unless she's actually a powerful swordswoman in disguise, what harm is there showing her in? Call Little Jade."

Hong stifled a grin. She did not think of herself as "powerful," but she was confident that a well-aimed bunch of needles and darts would easily take care of all the guards.

Little Jade was brought. Her eyes widened at the sight of Hong.

"Why... why have you... did you find anything?"

"I'd like to see Mrs. Guo."

"Is there a problem with this maid?" a guard asked.

"Oh no, nothing at all." Little Jade took Hong's arm. "She's from the governor's house; she just wanted to see Mistress Guo. Come on, Hong. Mistress has been bored all day long, I'm sure she'd be glad to see you..."

Hong dipped a curtsy to the guards and followed Little Jade. She was surprised when the maid led her to the east side of the compound.

"Was Mrs. Guo's room in this area of the residence?"

"We moved," Little Jade said. "She said the west wing wasn't peaceful enough. Why, there's only a couple of servants who pass through all day! It's not like we're setting off firecrackers or anything. I told you, she's paranoid."

The east wing was actually nicer, in Hong's opinion. Tucked away behind a group of artificial rocks and bamboo, with a small pond and a wooden bridge, and a round-stone paved path leading to the building, it was almost like entering a different world. The rest of the Guo residence was too flashy and extravagant and well, just not as refined.

Mrs. Guo's new quarters consisted of a pretty two-storied building with black-lacquered doors and windows with intricate bamboo lattice-work. What arrested Hong's attention was not the elegance of the residence, but that four women ranging from late teens to middle-age were patrolling the entrance. Their attire—plain cotton robes with the bare minimum of ornaments—showed that they were no ordinary servants. One had two daggers fastened to her belt—she must be adept at fighting with both hands. Another had the hilt of a broad sword jutting from her back, which indicated that the sword was so heavy that it couldn't be strapped to her waist. But it was one young woman carrying an ordinary-looking sword that caught Hong's attention. It was Flying Swallow.

"Were they selected from the bodyguard competition?" she asked Little Jade.

"Where else could they be from? Mistress said that she was afraid of thieves taking the wrong route and ending up here instead. But if I were a thief, I certainly wouldn't choose *this* part. It's nice, but not half as magnificent as the parlour or the master's quarters."

The inside was tastefully furnished. A beautiful, expensive-looking screen stand with exquisite gold-and-silver embroidery stood in a corner. A porcelain vase filled with fresh flowers was placed on a polished table top. Everything was sparkling clean, possibly to prevent the expecting mother from catching any germs.

Mrs. Guo was reclining on a low couch covered with cream-silk cushions. A ceramic bowl, half filled with rice and chicken, and a pair of chopsticks were set near her. She looked surprised when Hong and Little Jade entered.

Hong curtsied. "Good afternoon, Mrs. Guo. I hope that you have been doing better since we last met." It was a lie, however. Mrs. Guo's eyes bore a hollow, dejected look, and her cheeks were sallow and colourless. She looked as though she hadn't eaten for a long time.

"You're... aren't you Lynn's maid? Have you come with a message from her?"

"Yes," Hong said, deciding to use her mistress as an excuse for now. "There is something important that I must tell you."

"Is it about Fang?" Mrs. Guo said anxiously. "I've told her, I've talked to Father but he wouldn't listen to me."

"It isn't just that. I have come to ask for your insight in something else," Hong said. Slowly, she quoted, "'*Your eyes shine more beautifully than the diamonds on your throat...*'"

Mrs. Guo's face suddenly became ashen. "Wh... what did you just say?"

"A line of poetry, Mistress," Little Jade said, her expression clueless. "Is the poetry so very bad?"

"Little Jade." Mrs. Guo's voice was gentle yet firm. "Kindly drop by the market and fetch me some chrysanthemum tea, would you? I feel a headache coming."

"But Mistress, won't jasmine tea do? The chrysanthemum tea always has a long queue."

"I prefer chrysanthemums."

"All right." Little Jade gave in. "Shall I call in Little Emerald and Little Plum to wait upon you while I'm gone?"

"No. Hong will keep me company. If there's the need, she will call the others to help me."

Once Little Jade departed, Mrs. Guo told Hong to close the door securely and lock it.

"Who are you?" she said, pinning her with a searching look. "Did you come... on his behalf? Have you come to deliver a message from him? I've made it quite clear to him that I *won't* leave the Guos."

"I have no idea what your Ladyship is talking about," Hong said calmly. "I merely got the poem from Opal's younger brother. It strikes me as peculiar that a servant maid should receive a love poem tucked away in an ancient scroll, so I came to ask you."

"Opal?" Mrs. Guo still looked suspicious. "What does Opal have anything to do with it?"

"Have you not gifted your maid old scrolls with prefaces written by famous poets?"

"Never. Opal knows nothing of poetry. I have never given her anything—she could buy everything she needed from her wages. Why do you ask?"

Hong related what she had heard at Opal's family. Mrs. Guo stared.

"But... I don't understand... why would he give Opal those books? It doesn't make sense. And now that Opal is dead..."

Hong didn't understand either. "Who is this 'he' Your Ladyship refers to?"

Mrs. Guo hesitated. "No… no one of importance."

"Then do you have any idea where Opal got her poetry scrolls from? The ones that she used to pay off the debt of her family? It seems strange that she would have access to those things, if your Ladyship did not bestow them."

"I…" Mrs. Guo bit her lip and looked around. "All… all right. Since you are so concerned about saving your master, I'll tell you. But it won't make any difference. I may not even survive the day after."

Hong was astonished. "What do you mean? Why is your life in danger?"

"Play something for me." Mrs. Guo pointed to a lute in the corner. Lowering her voice, she whispered, "I do not wish others to know."

Hong understood immediately. Not only would the lute music blot out their voices, but it would also offer her an excuse for her visit. She crossed to the end of the room, picked up the lute, and started strumming a tune.

"It started when I was a child," Mrs. Guo said, averting her eyes. "I had a friend brought up in a good family of scholars. We played games, we shared meals, we had outings in the park. He asked me to marry him when we were ten, and I said yes." A pink flush stained her cheeks—for a second she looked remarkably beautiful, justifying her reputation.

"But Father didn't approve of him. My… ex-lover… was talented, but he could also be very emotional. I admired his verses, but sometimes he scared me with his mood swings. He was not exactly poor, but he was unlikely to provide for me indefinitely. When I was fifteen, Father forbade him to visit me anymore, unless he came accompanied by his nanny. Opal helped me; she arranged clandestine meetings for us at a secret hiding place while Yao stood watch."

Opal and Yao. Both of them dead.

"It wasn't easy." Mrs. Guo wiped tears from her eyes. "I was so afraid of being caught. Father can be extremely strict. Finally, my ex-lover said he was going to the capital to take the scholar exams. If he received the highest scores and offered a position at court, it would be easier for him to ask for my hand. But he failed. Opal told me that he was sick during travelling and didn't perform to the best of his abilities. But I knew. When I was younger, I thought he was incredibly talented, but after all these years of schooling, I knew that he wasn't as brilliant as he thought. He might have done better if he had studied harder, but he was, well, egoistical. And so his ability remained mediocre.

"When he failed the exams, he was devastated. I knew there was no hope for us. He tried to see me once, to convince me to elope with him. I refused, but he wouldn't give up. One day, Opal told me that Yao gave him a sound thrashing, which made him stop bothering me. I felt horribly sorry—Opal said Yao had broken a couple of ribs—so I risked the wrath of my father and went to see him. But when I arrived, his house was empty. The neighbours told me that the old nanny who brought him up had taken him to District Hwa-Lu; she had family there."

It was becoming clearer to Hong now. So this was the reason behind Opal's and Yao's deaths. They

had most likely extracted bribes from the ex-lover—
the poem in the valuable scrolls was the evidence—so
that he could meet Mrs. Guo in secret. Since he
eventually couldn't marry Mrs. Guo, he had come for
revenge. And he most probably had, by chance, come
by the Lost Manual. Old Man Liu had said anyone
could become powerful by learning the secret
techniques of the Manual.

"Well… it was over between us, obviously. So
when Father arranged the marriage with Merchant
Guo, I didn't object. I hadn't heard anything negative
about my husband. Though it did hurt when I finally
put on my red wedding gown and donned the
phoenix wedding headdress. I had believed that I
would grow up to marry my first love, but who knew
it would turn out like this?"

Mrs. Guo coughed; she had talked for some
time. Hong quickly set her lute aside and poured her
some water before resuming the song.

"Thank you." Mrs. Guo dabbed her eyes with a
silken handkerchief. "I thought I had put him out of
my life, but he came back. He found that I was
married, and tried to break in to the Guo residence. It
was fortunate that because the compound was so
huge, he didn't find me immediately. In fact, the dogs
were alerted and started barking. He got away, but
also stole some jewellery as well. I didn't know that it
was him at that time, however. It wasn't until I saw
him during the Cold Food Festival that I knew."

Hong struck a discordant note on the lute.
When Mrs. Guo had suddenly fell sick, Hong had
assumed it was due to her pregnancy. Could her
sickness have been triggered by the sudden

appearance of her ex-lover? Hong still remembered how white and trembling she had been.

"When everyone's attention was drawn to the boats, someone put his hand over my mouth and dragged me behind the tree. I couldn't believe it was him. He was changed, oh, he looked so... so *bitter*. He asked that I come away with him. I told him no, I was with child, but he wouldn't listen. As long as I promised to leave my husband, he'd forgive me for turning my back on him. He was going to drag me away, but I happened to throw up violently. And there were too many people in the park. He decided not to risk it.

"'Seven days. I'll give you seven days to make up your mind. I will penetrate the walls of your residence and find you.' And he picked up a fist-sized rock from the ground, held it for a moment, and the rock turned into dust. As he scattered the dust before me, he said, 'This is what I am capable of. Whatever bodyguards you hire, will their heads be harder to destroy than this rock?'

"He left. I didn't know what to do. I couldn't find out where he was without owning up to my past. All I could do was beg for my father-in-law to employ more proetection. It wasn't hard to convince him, because I could be carrying the first son for the Guo family."

The last note of the song faded away, as though echoing with her words.

Silence fell over the room. Then Hong spoke.

"So he will come tonight?"

"He will." There was no hesitation in Mrs. Guo's voice, only a weary resignation.

Hong thought hard. There was no time to conduct a search in the city—even if there were, to find a man within tens of thousands was impossible. The only solution was to confront him tonight and make him surrender.

Yet this was no simple task either. Hong was uncertain that she could do better than Yao. She had never personally witnessed the power of the Lost Manual, but from her *sifu's* description, she wasn't sure that she could kill the ex-lover, even when armed with her flying weapons and the newly acquired hollowed pens.

There were other bodyguards present; surely the ex-lover couldn't make it past them. And Mrs. Guo had changed her residence. He might not even make it to her quarters without confronting the dozen or so skilled fighters.

But Hong also needed to confront him, to question him about the Lost Manual. Old Man Liu was desperate to find it. What if the ex-lover didn't relent? What if he chose to bargain with her instead? Or in the worst-case scenario, what if she was no match for the Lost Manual and got killed in the process? She wouldn't know unless she tried.

"Let me stay here for one night," Hong said. "I will also stand guard for you."

Mrs. Guo put a hand over her mouth. "Why? Why are you doing this for me?"

"Because this man is very likely the same person who killed Opal and Yao. If he is caught, then Opal's husband will know that his wife's murderer is brought to justice. Moreover, my master Fang will be cleared of his name and released from jail. Also my friend Mr. Liu."

"You have no idea of his strength," Mrs. Guo said, her lip trembling. "Besides, we have found a good number of new bodyguards. If they cannot protect me, what more can you do? I know you are worried about your master, but honestly, this is unnecessary."

"I'm sure what he did was no more than some form of black magic," Hong lied. "I once met a Taoist priest who taught me how to deal with black magic. Your ex-lover threatens, but he is no more than a paper tiger. I will handle him."

She laid down the lute. She did not look like a servant at all, with her iron-like resolve in front of a woman who was much higher in rank. Mrs. Guo opened her mouth for a second, hesitated, and firmly pressed her lips together. This was no time for questions.

"Please send a servant to the governor's to tell them I am not returning until tomorrow," Hong said. "And now, let us work out a plan to protect you tonight."

24

There were advantages to masquerading as a pregnant woman, Hong found out. The loose folds of Mrs. Guo's robes provided perfect concealments for her weapons. Although she had not brought much with her when arriving at the Guo residence, it was easy to find makeshift weapons in the lady's room. Hairpins with sharp edges, not to mention needles from the pincushion, a couple of ink stones on the desk. Speaking of ink stones... Hong brought out the hollowed pens and laid them on the desk. They might come in handy when dealing with a murderer who had mastered an ancient power.

She paused to look at her reflection in the mirror. She was of a slenderer build than Mrs. Guo, obviously, but dressed up in the lady's fine clothes and having her hair done in the style of a married woman, plus the dim light of oil lamps at night—she hoped that the killer wouldn't discover that she was fake.

Mrs. Guo probably suspected that she was no ordinary servant maid. But what could Hong do to catch the murderer? It was either walk away or risk Mrs. Guo's suspicion. Besides, she would be leaving the governor's place soon.

Hong touched her cheek. It was heavily made up with perfumed face powders and rouge made from vermilion. She had taken liberties with Mrs. Guo's makeup box and tried to paint her face to resemble the magistrate's daughter. It wasn't easy. Mrs. Guo was a natural beauty; even without makeup, her features were symmetrical and perfect. But Hong had to apply cosmetics to make herself look more attractive. She knew well enough that she was no beauty, but sufficient makeup could enhance her otherwise average features. If one did not look closely, or dwelt on her voice and music, she might pass for a beauty.

And yet, her heart whispered, and yet the young master still wanted her. The thought of him still incarcerated fuelled her resolve. Hong made sure her weapons were all intact and sat down beside the table, her back facing the window.

She would catch the killer tonight.

Mrs. Guo was huddled in a small adjacent room on the second floor. Flying Swallow had been assigned to protect her. Although Hong would have liked to have all four women guarding Mrs. Guo, it would seem strange if there were no guards on the first floor. She hoped the remaining two guards would hold off the killer—but she doubted it. Since the killer had been in the compound before, he would know how to find his way and evade attacks.

According to Mrs. Guo, Flying Swallow was easily the best fighter during the recruiting competitions. Hong had to mask her emotions and pretend she had never seen Flying Swallow before, though inwardly she was glad to meet the swordswoman in person.

"Mrs. Guo will be safe with me." Flying Swallow spoke as though she was stating a fact instead of making a promise. Her gaze raked over Hong in an appraising manner. "Though I am sure you have your own methods."

The tone of her voice implied that she had discerned Hong's real ability. For those truly skilled, they could distinguish whether a person was trained in martial arts or not. The way an expert martial artist moved—precise, calculating, deft—would not escape another trained eye.

"I do," Hong replied, in an equally confident voice. "I've heard you are highly proficient in fighting. May I know how long you have trained?"

"Since I was young," Flying Swallow answered, but did not offer further details. "For a long time, I have relied on my fighting skills for survival."

Hong wondered what it was like to be a wandering swordswoman. She would likely follow the same path when she left the Shue household, travelling from city to city, often sleeping in deserted huts or even under trees, using her martial arts to right wrongs and bring justice. Flying Swallow seemed to enjoy her freedom, though she did look a bit lonely. Would her life also be the same?

Flying Swallow soon disappeared into the adjacent room where Mrs. Guo hid. Hong heard the sound of a lever being pulled down.

215

With Flying Swallow's presence, Hong worried less for Mrs. Guo's safety. But for her own…

The wind chimes outside clinked softly. Hong's trained ears picked up the faint thud of something hitting the ground—was it a body? Another thud followed. A cat hissed and leaped away.

Could it be the killer? Hong's knuckles turned white as she gripped the edge of the table. Yet she dared not stand up and go to the window. She could be found out impersonating Mrs. Guo.

Footsteps, as light as a feather, were coming from the stairway. Hong braced herself and prayed that the killer wouldn't go to the other room. While she trusted Flying Swallow to hold him off until she came to the rescue, she didn't want to think what he'd do when he saw Mrs. Guo.

The door creaked open.

Someone stepped in.

"I am touched," a male voice said. "You promised to wait for me. So I have come."

Hong recognised the voice. All the nerves in her body were stretched to a breaking point.

"Why do you not answer, my love? Come, let me take you out of this miserable place. We shall be together forever."

Hong rose. The scarves around her sleeves rustled against her skirts.

"A romantic offer, but I am afraid I must decline," she said, facing him squarely. "Calligrapher Pai."

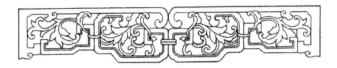

25

It was indeed the young man who had set up stall in the market, who had written Shu-Mo's love letters. He was dressed completely in black, his hair bound up in a black cloth as well, but his features were easily recognisable. Now it was clear. He was Mrs. Guo's ex-lover. The pieces were falling into place. Hong suddenly realised why he had managed to sabotage the boats earlier and appear on the outing. They had been near his stall, talking about going to the Cold Food Festival with Mrs. Guo. He had heard them, probably after his unsuccessful attempt to infiltrate the Guo residence, and decided to waylay Mrs. Guo at the park instead. The magistrate's daughter rarely left her quarters—hence it was an excellent opportunity.

"Who are you?" he growled. "How dare you impersonate my Wen-Jun?"

Hong used that precious moment of his amazement to her advantage. A flourish of her sleeve, and a rain of needles shot out, aiming for every vital point of his body.

Pai's eyes widened, but he reacted fast enough. Both of his palms hit out; the air seemed to swirl and converge into a wall. The needles met with invisible resistance and fell down on the floor.

So this was the power of the Water Fist. Remarkable. Quite the antithesis of her flying weapons. One blow—he didn't even have to make contact with skin—and she couldn't even hurt him. For the first time in her life, Hong felt useless. How was she going to defeat him when her flying weapons weren't working?

"Where—is—she?" Calligrapher Pai said, his expression no longer the friendly, harmless young man in the market.

Hong kept her expression blank. "You also killed her servant Opal and the fighter Yao, did you not? Why didn't you just seek the magistrate's daughter out? What did her servants do to you?"

Pai narrowed his eyes. "It was their fault. If they hadn't stood in the way of my pursuing Wen-Jun, she would have consented to elope with me! That money-loving maid made me bribe her for meetings—those poetry scrolls were my family heirlooms! When I sought her, she told me she had already pawned them off to pay for her father's debts! And that nasty guard beat the hell out of me when I requested one last visit to say goodbye. I was mad, but I was helpless at that time. Now I can exact revenge." He stared at his hand with a maniac glint. "How sweet it is! They treated me like horse manure, they deserved to die."

"But how did you kill them? Yao was known to be invincible." Hong hoped to extract the information of the Lost Manual from him.

"Invincible my foot," Pai sneered. "With the secret powers I have, nothing can stop me. Not even you."

With that last remark, he lashed out at her. All he did was raise both his hands and push his palms out, and Hong could feel his force emanating in waves, so strong and suffocating that she was certain to die instantly if she was close enough.

Hong sailed to a corner of the room; the power of the Water Fist hit the screen stand behind her, burning through the thick white paper and destroying the beautiful landscapes painted on it. A second later, the screen collapsed in a heap of bamboo and paper.

There was nowhere to hide now.

Hong readied her poisonous darts again, eight of them wedged in the eight spaces between her fingers, and sent them flying towards Pai.

The former scholar hit out. This time the force was so strong that the darts were sent flying in various directions, one heading for her throat. Hong drew out the dagger in her boot and ping! The dart clanged against the dagger's sheath and fell on the floor. The next second, Hong also dropped the dagger with a small cry of pain. The force that rebounded from her own dart was so strong that it penetrated the dagger and hit her wrist.

"Tell me where you hid her," Pai growled, advancing on her. "Or I'll kill you. Your baubles are useless against me."

She didn't doubt it. Her head was hurting from the turbulence. Her darts were all used up. Not to mention that any weapon she aimed at him would simply be swept up by his force, or even worse, be forced to change direction.

Hong scrambled backwards until her back met the wall. A trickle of perspiration ran down her forehead. If she didn't act fast—she'd end up the same way as Yao did.

Yet, as she observed the way he moved, there might be something she could use to her advantage. He was strong, no doubt, stronger than ten men combined, but he was not a trained fighter. He had no idea how to duck or dodge, or how to calculate his opponent's strengths and weaknesses. His hands might unleash powers she could never withstand, but what about other parts of his body?

She had to find a way to harm him without being hit.

He was closer now, his arm raised to deliver a final fatal blow...

Hong rolled over the ground, snatched up one of the hollowed pens lying on the ground, and shot at Pai's ankle.

Pai let out a grunt of pain; the bloody needle point jutted out of his flesh. Knowing that it might take some time for the poison to take effect, she scooped her fallen dagger and threw it at him.

"Aaaaah!" Pai cried. The dagger was stuck in his arm; blood dripped on the ground, splattering the beautifully polished floor. Since he relied on the force delivered by his hands, half of his power was already gone.

Now it was her chance. Hong sprang up, darted forward, and with a fluid motion, disjointed his other wrist. With one hand bleeding and the other injured, Pai was no longer a threat.

Hong took off her largest hairpin; it was made of iron and the end was sharp enough to cause major damage. She held the hairpin against his throat. One jab and he could bleed to death.

"Where did you learn this power?"

Silence.

Hong let the pin graze his flesh. A tiny trickle of blood ran down his throat.

Pai gave a twisted grin. "I… if she does not come with me, I'd rather die."

"Don't be absurd. She is married and with child."

"She is *mine*."

Shouts came from outside. Whatever method Pai had used to enter the Guo household, the guards seemed to be finally discovering it now.

"Listen," Hong said quickly. "I might be able to save your life if you tell me how you gained possession of the Lost Manual. Otherwise, you will certainly forfeit your life."

Pai seemed not to hear her. He stood transfixed; the wounds on his body were enough to make one scream and writhe, but he concentrated only on a figure at the door.

Mrs. Guo, accompanied by Flying Swallow, was looking down at them with absolute horror.

"My… Wen… Jun…" Pai croaked, reaching a broken arm to her. Suddenly, he seemed to regain his power. A strong force radiated from his body, throwing Hong off course.

He advanced towards Mrs. Guo as swiftly as his needle-pierced ankle would allow.

Mrs. Guo screamed. Indeed, he was no longer the refined, well-dressed scholar whom a young girl might admire. His eyes were glowing like a wild beast, and blood was streaming profusely from his left arm, leaving a bloody trail behind him.

The next second, Pai stopped. As swift as a fleeing deer, Flying Swallow darted in front of Mrs. Guo and drove a sword into his chest. Meanwhile, Hong had grabbed another hollow pen and sent a long needle into the back of his neck.

And so the murderer of Yao and Opal, the besotted lover of the magistrate's daughter, the once-brilliant scholar who was predicted a promising future, crashed on the floor. He twitched a bit, and then moved no more.

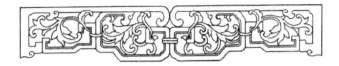

26

Although Pai had been revealed to be the murderer, Hong's troubles were far from being over. She still had to ensure Fang and Meng-Ting would be safely released, so right after Pai drew his last breath, she made a deal with Mrs. Guo.

"Since I have saved your life from this monster, you would do well to repay me by telling your father to release my young master and my friend at once. Pai admitted that he killed Yao and Opal. Now that the real murderer is found, the innocent should not be kept behind bars any longer."

Mrs. Guo, who was barely recovering from her shock, could only nod.

Then there was the issue of the Lost Manual. After making sure that Calligrapher Pai did not carry anything resembling a scroll or just anything with words written on it, Hong had to again call for the help of Old Man Liu's network of beggar spies. She couldn't be combing the city all day long. Besides, she was feeling rather worn out from the battle with Pai. Although she was not seriously injured, the turbulent wave-like power he released had made her nauseous and occasionally she found it hard to breathe. When Meng-Ting was released, she would ask him for a diagnosis.

Two days after Pai's death, Hong rose a bit later than usual. Partly because she was not fully recovered from Pai's impact, partly because Governor Shue had not yet returned from the capital, so her morning chores would not take a long time.

Hong sat down on the small bamboo stool in front of her mirror. Her long black hair cascaded down her back, framing her pale face. Although she was capable of doing complicated makeup, this was what she usually preferred. No ornaments, no styling... it made her feel light and relaxed and carefree. Too bad that her life rarely afforded her such moments.

A knock on the door, and Golden Lotus entered.

"Did you hear the news?" Golden Lotus perched herself on a chair. "Young Master Fang has been cleared! They say the real murderer has been caught! You wouldn't believe it!"

Hong did her best to appear surprised. "Who did it?"

"Well, be prepared to hear this: it's that calligrapher Shu-Mo was paying to write his love letters! Pai is his name, and he used to live near the magistrate's old compound. It seemed that he tried to steal something valuable from the magistrate's, and Yao, who was working as the magistrate's bodyguard, caught him and gave him such a sound beating that Pai almost died."

No mention of Mrs. Guo. Hong wasn't sure how much the Guos knew of the magistrate's daughter's past with Calligrapher Pai, especially since he had been found dead in her quarters, but it seemed they were anxious to preserve Mrs. Guo's reputation. If it was known that Pai had been found dead at Mrs. Guo's quarters, plus the fact he was her ex-lover, it would look as though she had been carrying on an affair when she was already pregnant with her first child! No husband could tolerate such an insult, and no family could bear such a stain on their reputation. Particularly a large, well-to-do family like the Guos.

"How terrible."

"Ain't it so? Well, Pai got away for a while, recovered, and he returned to avenge himself. Little Jade said that he learnt some creepy black magic, which is how he managed to kill Yao. He also did a lot of stealing in the city, including Merchant Guo's residence. But Merchant Guo went out and hired several new bodyguards—one of them could perform spells to counter Yao's black magic. So when Yao tried to steal a second time, he met his end."

Hong felt like choking with laughter. So Mrs. Guo had used parts of her story about black magic. If only Golden Lotus knew the truth.

"So this means Young Master is free! I'm so glad, because I heard he was injured in prison."

"Injured?" Hong was alarmed. "Is it serious?"

"Shu-Mo said it wasn't anything to worry about; Young Master is as strong as a bull. But it *might* be much worse, if he continues to stay in that horrid place. Anyway, Shu-Mo said that Master Gwang and

Master Ping have gone to the prison and made sure things were all right."

"When is Master Fang returning?" Hong said. "And I assume Mr. Liu would be released as well?"

"Oh, it should be any day soon, they just need to get the paperwork done. Say, this merits a celebration! Let's get up a huge feast for Master Fang!"

"Why, of course," Hong said. "I'll go and buy the ingredients. I'll also need to pop in to *sifu's* to let him know his grandson would be all right, so I will be late."

She did not mention that she also had to question the beggar spies to see if they had uncovered anything new about Calligrapher Pai. She would have loved to visit Fang, but since he was no longer in danger and that his siblings were taking care of him, she would wait until he returned. Old Man Liu would want her to focus on searching for more clues on the Lost Manual.

It was just luck that Fang came home when Hong was absent. There was a tearful reunion when Lynn ran and threw herself in his arms, not caring if he smelled terrible. She only broke away when he let out a grunt of pain. The wounds that Ho Jiang-Min inflicted on him were still raw and painful. Gwang and Ping, who had finally resorted to pooling together a bribe for the magistrate, were relieved. They asked for the reasons for his release, which Fang was not quite sure of either, but apparently the real killer had been caught.

The next morning, Fang sat with his brothers in the main reception hall.

"Thank goodness your name is cleared," Gwang said. "I just knew that you couldn't have killed him."

Fang grinned, touched at his brother's words.

However, his brother continued, "Because there's no way you can overpower a prized fighter. You're not up to that level yet."

"Next time, if you want to help out your friend, you had better consult us first," Ping said. "Going to visit the fighter on your own! You'd better have more common sense."

"I know," Fang said, stung by his brother's condescending tone. "It was too rash of me, all right?"

"Though isn't it also strange that the killer was a mere scholar?"

"I only heard that the scholar had used some form of black magic," Ping said. "Do you think it was only an excuse? Perhaps the magistrate found him a better culprit than Fang."

Gwang frowned. "Sounds spooky. But the scholar's already dead, so we'd never know."

"I think it's because Ho Jiang-Min was carrying things too far." Ping looked thoughtful. "Even if it is legal to torture criminals into confession, the physician said that if your wounds weren't properly treated, the germs in the prison cell could enter your wounds and into your bloodstream. You could be seriously ill, or even be dead."

Gwang pound a fist on the table. "That scumbag! I'll give him a sound beating the next time I see him!"

"Don't," Fang said quickly. "Don't harm him unless necessary. Remember his status; he could make your life truly miserable if you're on his bad side."

"Anyway, what's important is that you're safely back." Ping poured a cupful of wine. "Here, it's Rose Daughter from Luo's Winehouse. Chow got a full jar once he learnt you're set free."

Fang sat back and drank the wine. He had seen Chow earlier and told him the truth. Chow had seemed resigned by now; though he was still in low spirits, he did not appear as dejected as before. Fang decided to find an occasion and invite him for a hunting excursion or a game of horse polo.

"Masters!" The steward ran inside. "Please follow me immediately! There is a royal messenger from the emperor!"

"A royal messenger? But Father isn't even back yet!"

"Come, let us go to the courtyard," Gwang said. "We shouldn't keep the royal messenger waiting."

In the courtyard, a middle-aged man dressed in dark purple robes was waiting for them. A small procession of servants and eunuchs stood behind him.

"For the Shue Family."

The three brothers bowed deeply. "We humbly await the emperor's command. May the emperor live in eternal peace and prosperity."

The messenger unfurled a handsome golden-edged scroll and read out: "The Illustrious Emperor His Excellency has arranged a marriage decision. To promote peace and strengthen ties within districts, His Excellency decrees that the eldest daughter of Governor Shue shall wed the eldest son of Governor

Ling-Hu. The marriage shall take place on an auspicious date in October."

The three brothers bowed again. "We thank His Excellency for his benevolent and wise decisions."

The messenger looked at them. "Which of you is the eldest?"

Gwang stepped forward. "I am."

The messenger placed the golden scroll in both of his hands.

"Will Your Honour join us for a cool drink?" Gwang said solicitously.

"A tempting offer, but I must be going," the messenger said, wiping sweat from his brow. "It is a long journey back to the palace."

When the messenger was gone, the three brothers stared at each other, speechless for a second.

"Well," Gwang said. "This *is* a surprise. Remember what Father said before he left for court?"

"I don't think this is a particularly well-made decision," Ping said. "Marriage alliances won't be sufficient to end strife and conflict between states."

Fang glared at the golden scroll, as though he wished he could rip it in shreds. "I have to tell Lynn."

He found his sister happily seated on a swing in the back yard. Her laughter rang out over the rocks and bamboo grove—blithe, carefree, full of joy. What would she say when she learnt the news?

"Master Fang!" Golden Lotus and Silver Peony spotted him and grinned. Golden Lotus was pushing Lynn, making her go higher on the swing, while Silver Peony was watering the peonies in the garden.

"Is there anything you wanted?" Silver Peony asked, running over to him. She still held a bamboo scoop in one hand, and a bamboo pail of water in the other.

"No, I'm all right." Fang focused his gaze on his sister. "Lynn, can you come down for a while? I have news for you." He glanced at the other two maids for a second, and raised his eyebrows.

Lynn understood. "Golden Lotus, Silver Peony, run along and see if the kitchen or laundry room needs any help. My dear brother is probably going to lecture me on frivolity again."

Once the maids were gone, Fang sat down on a smooth rock across from the swing.

"So what has been ailing my dear brother?" Lynn grinned at him. "Lady trouble? Listen, if you're still devising a method to make Hong notice you…"

"That's not why I came to talk to you," Fang said, though he had to return a wry grin. Things certainly weren't progressing between him and Hong either, but right now the emperor's decree was more important. "Lynn, the emperor's messenger was just here a while ago."

"Really?" Lynn tilted her head. "What can it be? Is the emperor ordering any of our brothers to be stationed at a distant post, like in the North? Or did he promote Father to a position at court? Urgh, I don't think I'd want to move inland, it's going to be so much colder in the winter."

Fang sighed. He placed a hand on her arm. "Lynn… the emperor has made you an offer of marriage."

"What?" Lynn's eyes were round like saucers. "I'm to become a concubine in his… his *harem*?"

"No! It's not like that! He has arranged a marriage for you. The groom is the Hwa-Lu governor's eldest son."

Lynn stared. She got off the swing and walked away.

"Sister!" Fang went after her and caught her arm. "Lynn, I know this is a huge shock for you, but it's the imperial command…"

She turned around, and he was pained to see tears brimming in her beautiful eyes.

"I know, I know, there's nothing we can do," she said, wiping her face fiercely. "It's just so *sudden*. I've always thought that Father would allow me several candidates to choose from, but now I have no choice. I have to do what the emperor says. It's all because of the stupid peace they're trying to maintain between districts, I suppose?"

"It is." Fang took her hand in his. "I'll do my best to help you, sis. I can't revoke the decree, but I can accompany you to District Hwa-Lu. Father would likely want one of us to go with you, so it might as well be me. I'll meet your future husband before the ceremony and make sure that he'll treat you well."

But he didn't sound very convincing. It was quite possible that the groom would be a good-for-nothing, like Magistrate Ho's despicable son. He might possess a bad temper, be fond of drinking and gambling, or even have a violent nature. But it was the emperor's order. There was nothing they could do.

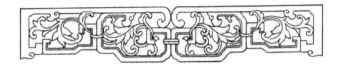

27

"Golden Lotus, can you hang up the clothes for me? I've already finished washing this load."

Hong set a basket of freshly washed laundry on the stone-paved ground.

"What's the hurry?" Golden Lotus asked. "Are you going to Old Man Liu's again?"

"No. I am going to see Young Master Fang. The robe you've been talking about... may I borrow it?"

"Oh! Of course, go right ahead! It's in the trunk under my bed." Golden Lotus reached out and patted Hong's arm. "So you've finally come to your senses?"

Hong blushed.

"Ah... getting shy, aren't we? Honestly, I don't see what you have to be nervous about. Shu-Mo said that Young Master has liked you since you were childhood friends. It's about time, I'd say."

About time to leave, in fact. Now that the murderer had been found, she should not stay any longer. Old Man Liu was planning to fabricate a story of another lute master who lived in Hwa-Lu District, so she could leave the Shue household and go to Hwa-Lu in search of the Lost Manual. Shue Song had promised that he would honour whatever decision she made.

Still… a pang of frustration and pain gnawed at her mind. Even though she had been mentally preparing herself for the eventual separation, she found it difficult to simply go and bid her young master goodbye. But it had to be done.

The robe that Golden Lotus wanted to lend her was elegant and lovely—pale yellow upper sleeves, apple-green skirt, and a flowing white sash that almost fell to the floor. It *was* more revealing than the dark blue robe she used to wear every day, but since Golden Lotus used to say the cut of her robe resembled a nun's, any other outfit would be easily considered spicier.

She applied a light layer of scented cream, re-painted her eyebrows, and inserted a single jade hair pin in her hair. No other ornament—she wanted to look nice, but not too dressed up.

Hong picked up her lute and headed for the garden.

She was slightly surprised to see Fang with his sister, instead of spending his time with his elder brothers or sparring with the soldiers. Lynn seemed to be upset about something, and Fang had his arm around her shoulders, obviously trying to comfort her.

Hong wondered if she should go back. But when she paused, Fang happened to lift his head.

"Hong? Are you going to Old Man Liu's?"

"I…" Hong swallowed. "Welcome home, Master Fang. I thought I'd play one song, if you weren't busy…"

Fang started. It was the first time she had volunteered to play for him.

"But of course," Lynn said, rising from the bench. "I think I'd better go back to my room now. My makeup must be a mess now."

She wiped at her face and hurried away.

"Forgive me if I'm intruding, but is Mistress Lynn all right? She usually is so carefree."

Fang sighed. "We just received the imperial messenger. The emperor has decreed that Lynn should marry the eldest son of the Hwa-Lu Governor."

"Hwa-Lu?" The beggar spies had told her that Calligrapher Pai was staying at District Hwa-Lu before he returned to the city.

"I suppose they're trying to maintain peace between the districts. We haven't heard much of the Hwa-Lu governor, but I'm going to accompany Lynn to her wedding. To make sure that her prospective groom is good enough for her."

Fang tried to sound optimistic, but he felt his tone was falling flat. Even if the Hwa-Lu governor's son was a good-for-nothing, what could he do? The emperor's decree was the law.

"Do not worry, Young Master," Hong said gently. "Mistress Lynn is the daughter of Master Shue. Moreover, she isn't the kind of woman who would let herself be treated badly."

"I know." Fang rubbed his forehead. "Still, it is troubling news for her. She always thought she'd have a say in her future, but now it's decided for her." He looked at her, and something changed in his expression. "Are these... new clothes?"

Hong blushed. "Golden Lotus kindly lent it to me. I thought... maybe a celebration... something different..."

"You should wear this more often," Fang blurted. Hesitantly, he reached out and put his hand over hers. This time, she didn't back away, didn't shy away from his touch. Was it compassion after his imprisonment, or was she beginning to feel differently towards him?

His heart pounding, Fang leaned closer. "Hong, would you like to..."

A voice interrupted them. Ping, his arms crossed, strode towards the bench.

"Fang, come here for a second. Father has returned and heard of the news."

If Ping had invited him on a hunt, Fang would have refused. But he couldn't refuse to see his father, especially when there was the marriage decision concerning Lynn.

"He wants all of us in the office. Now."

Reluctantly, Fang removed his hand from Hong's and stood up.

A few days later, Hong went to see her *sifu* to give an update on their search of the Lost Manual. Meng-Ting, who was newly released from prison, also dropped by with some herbal medicine. Due to the advent of autumn, Old Man Liu had developed a cold. Despite gruff protests that his cold would soon be gone, Meng-Ting wasn't reassured and insisted on bringing more medicine.

"I have failed you, *sifu*. When I tried to get him to reveal where the Manual was, he chose to take his own life instead. I also searched the inn he stayed at and his old house, but nothing turned up."

"Hmph. Did you ask the innkeeper? The other guests?"

"I did my best. But it is hard when the inn receives numerous guests every day. I did find out that he came from District Hwa-Lu."

"Isn't that where the governor's daughter is going?" Meng-Ting said. "It's all over the city that the emperor ordered Lady Lynn to wed the eldest son of the Hwa-Lu governor."

"What a coincidence!" Old Man Liu said. "This wedding—you say that it takes place in District Hwa-Lu?"

"Yes."

"And you just said that Pai came from the same place?"

"It is the place he went to after he was nearly beaten to death by Yao."

"Excellent!" Old Man Liu barked. "Hong, this is your chance. You are to offer to accompany Shue's daughter to Hwa-Lu. While you are there, use the opportunity to look around. See if you can find anything on Pai."

Hong's heart leaped. She would not have to leave the Shue family—not yet. Fang had said he was going to accompany Lynn to Hwa-Lu. She could still spend some time with him—it might make her eventual farewell more painful, but right now she didn't care.

"But Grandpa," Meng-Ting said hesitantly. "Servant maids who accompany their ladies are

236

usually regarded as—er—additional concubines for the groom. It's the custom. What if the Hwa-Lu governor's son claims Hong as his?"

"No matter." Liu was unconcerned with worldly manners. "Hong will find a way out. Right?"

Hong bowed her head.

"Yes, *sifu*."

A WORD FROM THE AUTHOR

Thanks for reading! If you enjoyed the book, please help other readers enjoy it too by leaving a review online. Of course, Hong's story doesn't end here. Will she find the Lost Manual at District Hwa-Lu? Can Fang make further progress in his courting Hong? To learn when the next book will be released, please sign up for my mailing list at http://www.ayaling.com.

~Aya~

*If you'd like to learn about other stuff I've written, including a FREE book, please turn to the next page.

~PRINCESSES DON'T GET FAT~

A fairy tale romance with a plus-sized heroine and plenty of dessert.

Princess Valeria of Amaranta is fat, but she doesn't care. All she wants to do is to eat and lead an idle life. When it becomes apparent she cannot get a husband, her mother decides to send her to the Royal Riviera Academy of Fighting Arts. For a chubby princess who has never picked up a sword, life at the Academy is torture. Worst of all, the food is terrible.

Valeria decides to improve Rivieran cuisine by sneaking into the palace kitchens and offering her expertise, never expecting the crown prince would take interest in her kitchen excursions. As they spend more time together, the princess must decide whether she should become thin or stay in the kitchens with her beloved food and remain fat.

*Princesses Don't Get Fat is currently a FREE ebook at most online vendors. Visit my website at http://www.ayaling.com for more information!

~PRINCESSES DON'T FIGHT IN SKIRTS~

Who says a girl can't wear a dress and wield a sword?

It has become fashionable now for princesses to run away and seek adventure. Princess Arianna of Linderall, however, is willing to stay home and be proper. She screams when she sees spiders, enjoys sewing and dancing, and always looks at her reflection first thing in the morning.

What happens when her great aunt, the first woman warrior in history, decides that Ari is too "traditional" and sends her off to the Royal Rivieran Academy of Fighting Arts? Can she survive the vigorous physical training and earn the respect of her peers? Moreover, can she attract the attention of a prince even when she's forced to relinquish makeup and dresses during training?

ABOUT THE AUTHOR

Aya is from Taiwan, where she struggles daily to contain her obsession with mouthwatering and unhealthy foods. Often she will devour a good book instead. Her favourite books include martial arts romances, fairy tale retellings, high fantasy, cozy mysteries, and manga.

As a native Mandarin speaker, she has also created a series of Chinese vocabulary flashcards under the name of Tina Ling. If you, or someone you know, happen to be learning traditional Chinese characters, check them out at Tina's website (http://tradchinese.weebly.com/)!

Made in the USA
Middletown, DE
17 January 2016